Other Titles by Jackie French

Pharaoh

THE BOY WHO
CONQUERED
THE NILE

Jackie French

Angus&Robertson

An imprint of HarperCollins*Publishers*

Angus&Robertson
An imprint of HarperCollins*Publishers*, Australia

First published in Australia in 2007
by HarperCollins*Publishers* Australia Pty Limited
ABN 36 009 913 517
www.harpercollins.com.au

HarperCollins*Publishers*
25 Ryde Road, Pymble, Sydney NSW 2073, Australia
31 View Road, Glenfield, Auckland 10, New Zealand
77–85 Fulham Palace Road, London W6 8JB, United Kingdom
2 Bloor Street East, 20th Floor, Toronto, Ontario, M4W 1A8, Canada
10 East 53rd Street, New York NY 10022, USA

French, Jackie.
  Pharaoh: the boy who conquered the Nile.
  For children.
  ISBN 13: 978 0 2072 0082 3.
  ISBN 10: 0 2072 0082 3.
  I. Title.
A823.3

Cover image of boy: photography and styling by Samantha Everton; costume design by
Larry Edwards, the Magic Wardrobe, Melbourne; model: Johnny Hajj
Cover images of lynx (by Sivolob Or), crocodile (by Alistair Cotton) and Nile River
landscape (by Efremova Irina Alexeevna) © Shutterstock
Cover image of cobra (by Tim Flach) © Getty Images
Cover design by Darren Holt, HarperCollins Design Studio
Maps by Darren Holt, HarperCollins Design Studio
Typeset in 11.5/15.5pt ACaslon Regular by Helen Beard, ECJ Australia Pty Ltd
Printed and bound in Australia by Griffin Press
60gsm Bulky Paperback used by HarperCollins*Publishers* is a natural, recyclable product
made from wood grown in a combination of sustainable plantation and regrowth
forests. It also contains up to a 20% portion of recycled fibre. The manufacturing
processes conform to the environmental regulations in Tasmania, the place of
manufacture.

7 6   08 09 10

To Nina and Patrick — this adventure
is for you!
Much love, Jackie

THE MIDDLE EAST AROUND 3000 BCE

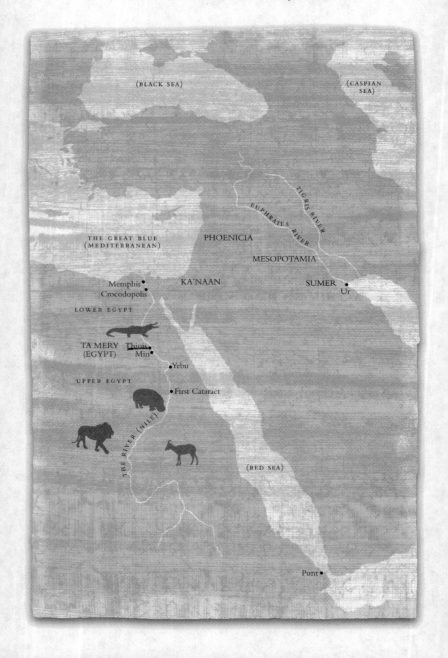

THE MIDDLE EAST AROUND 2000 CE

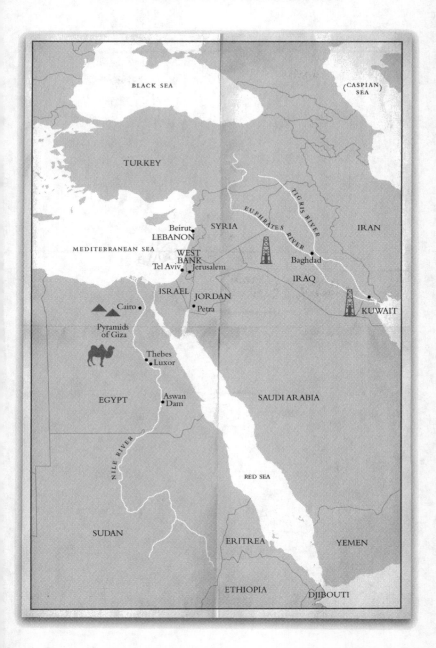

CHAPTER 1

The Season of Flood (Early Autumn)

On one side of the cliff was the Endless Desert, a land of wadies, heat and rock. On the other side the dark flood spread across the valley, bringing the rich black soil that fed the land along the River.

Narmer loved it up on the cliff. He could see his whole world from here: the town of Thinis, safe from the flood within its high mud dyke, and its fields, still covered by the silt-laden waters, smooth as polished tiles except for the white froth at their edges.

Hapi, god of the River's flood, had sent his people a good flood this year. It had risen sixteen cubits, up to the twentieth measuring stair by the palace walls. A small flood, or none at all, meant famine. A giant flood washed across the dykes, sweeping away houses, orchards, animals and people.

But this flood had been perfect. A sign that the King and his sons had pleased the gods.

Narmer was his father's heir. He and the King were responsible for the land's Ma'at, or wellbeing.

Narmer grinned. Except when he escaped for a day by himself.

He glanced down at the two lizards strung onto the belt of his kilt. Not much to show for a day's hunting. But Ra the sun god was beginning to sail his ship down the sky. High time to head home. His father would forgive a day spent hunting, but he'd be genuinely angry if Narmer were late to greet their guests.

Narmer broke into a jog, the dry desert wind washing across his face, spiced with the scent of flood.

'Hail, Prince Narmer!'

Narmer stopped. He peered down into the wadi where the sound had come from. But there was nothing except a wildcat sitting in the shadows, as tall as his knees perhaps, its fur the same colours as the rock and shadows, a patchwork of orange and black.

It was the fattest cat he'd ever seen.

The wildcat regarded him lazily. Narmer lifted his spear. The skin would make a fine mat for his floor. But then the words came again.

'Hail, Prince Narmer!'

Narmer felt his skin prickle. How could a cat talk? Magic? Or maybe it was a demon! One of the palace women had told him the Sand People's tale of the afreets who roamed the Endless Desert, sucking the life out of unwary hunters. He grasped his spears more firmly.

The cat licked one of its enormous paws and began to clean its tufted ears. Why wasn't it afraid of a boy with spears?

Magic or demon, this needed to be investigated. Narmer began to climb into the wadi. A few stones trickled downward as his bare feet half slid down its slope.

The wildcat was washing its nose now. He could smell it

from here: <u>a musky scent, not unpleasant, of fur and wild animal.</u>

'Go no further, o great and wondrous Prince.'

It was a female voice, Narmer now realised. <u>It was beautiful, like water cascading down a wadi.</u>

But this time he had been watching the cat when the voice spoke, and its mouth hadn't opened. The voice had come from the rock just in front of him. From a sheer, smooth rock face ...

Narmer flung himself face down onto the stones of the gully. 'Great One! What should I call you? Are you a demon? A goddess?'

'Neither.' The voice sounded scornful.

'What, then?' demanded Narmer, still face down. 'What sort of creature speaks but is invisible?'

The voice was silent for a moment. And then it said, 'I am an oracle. You've heard of oracles, haven't you?'

'Of course.' Narmer kept his face against the ground. Seknut had told him about oracles too. They brought advice from the gods. But he'd never heard of an oracle near Thinis.

An oracle! Speaking to him!

'You may sit up now, o great king's son,' said the Oracle.

Narmer brushed some of the dust off his bare chest and kilt and sat upright. People had told him he was special all his life. But to speak to an oracle ...

'Does my father the King know about you?' he asked the rock. How did one address an oracle? 'O mighty Oracle,' he added, hoping he'd got it right.

'No,' replied the Oracle.

'How long have you been here?'

'Not long.'

'Then why have you come? Am I allowed to ask you questions?'

'I suppose so.' The Oracle didn't sound very concerned.

The cat was washing its whiskers now. Even if it couldn't speak, there was something eerie about a wild animal that showed no fear of people. But Narmer forced his voice to remain calm.

'What can you tell me, o Oracle?'

'Well,' said the Oracle slowly, 'You are the son of King Scorpion of Thinis, one of the most powerful towns along the River.'

'*The* most powerful,' corrected Narmer automatically — then wished he had held his tongue. Had he offended the Oracle?

'So sorry,' conceded the Oracle. To Narmer's relief she sounded almost amused. 'King of great and glorious Thinis, *the* most powerful town in the world.'

Narmer frowned. What was funny about saying that Thinis was the greatest town in the world? It held more than a thousand people! It was bigger than Yebu, twice as big as little towns like Min ...

'You are young, you are noble, you are handsome,' the Oracle continued. 'Your brother Prince Hawk is older than you. But the King chose you to rule the country after him.'

Narmer nodded impatiently.

'They call you the Golden One.' There was an almost bitter sound to the Oracle's words now. 'Beloved of your father, beloved of the people. The women exclaim as you walk past.'

The wildcat stretched and strolled towards Narmer, then sat down a spear's length away and stared at the dead lizards. Narmer shivered. He had never been so close to a wild animal before — not a live one, anyway. But he wasn't scared of a wildcat, he told himself, no matter how large it was or how strangely it behaved.

'Um ... does the cat belong to you?' he asked, trying to ignore its smell. 'To your shrine, I mean?'

The oracle giggled. It sounded like a chord played on a lyre. Narmer had never realised that oracles giggled. 'Cats belong to themselves. But it stays near me, if that's what you mean. Throw it one of your lizards,' she commanded. 'That's what it's waiting for.'

Narmer untied the longer of the two lizards and threw it at the cat. The cat placed one heavy paw on the lizard's tail, then ripped its head clean off. Narmer could hear the crunch of bones as the great animal chewed.

Slurp ... the cat licked out the entrails.

Narmer stared at the massive animal. Was he really here, speaking to an oracle and watching a wildcat gnaw at one of his lizards? But it was true. And if an oracle had decided to speak to him it was time he found out something useful.

'Please tell me something I don't know, o mighty Oracle,' said Narmer quietly.

'Er ... what do you wish to know, o great Prince, beloved son of Thinis?'

'My future.'

'Ah,' said the Oracle, 'that's easy. You're going to be King of Thinis. And in two new moons' time you'll marry the beautiful <u>Berenib, Princess of Yebu,</u> may she live as long as the River and her face never lose its bloom.'

Yebu was nearly as big as Thinis. Marrying Berenib would help keep peace between the two kingdoms.

'Is she beautiful?' asked Narmer. 'I've never seen her.'

'Princesses are always beautiful,' said the Oracle. 'At least, if you're wise you say they are. Is there anything else you want to know?'

'Everything! Will there be peace? War? A long life? Will I have sons?' Narmer had never thought about all this before, but suddenly he wanted to know.

'All of those,' said the Oracle shortly. 'And one final thing ...'

'What?'

'It's time for you to go home. You are supposed to meet the trader from the north this afternoon — or had you forgotten?'

'Of course not.'

How could he have forgotten the Trader? He and his porters had arrived late last night, tired and dusty. They had still been asleep in the palace guesthouse when Narmer left that morning.

Other traders came along the River, carrying <u>ebony wood, or ostrich feathers, or lion skins to trade for Thinis's grain</u>. But this trader had come across the Endless Desert! No trader had come that way since the time of Narmer's grandfather. What would the Trader look like? Narmer wondered. <u>Would he have black skin like the southerners?</u> Or look even stranger, like the <u>slave with eyes like the sky</u> whom a trader from the <u>Delta</u> had brought last year?

'You don't want to offend the Trader by being late,' said the Oracle firmly. 'You've never seen treasures like the Trader carries! All the glories from beyond the furthest horizon! Worth all that the kingdom of Thinis can offer! Off you go, o great Prince Narmer, may your name be remembered for generations. But you may leave the other lizard for the cat.'

Narmer wasn't used to being dismissed. Even by an oracle. And there were so many questions he hadn't asked. Besides, he wanted to hear her voice again.

'May I come again, mighty Oracle? Tomorrow?'

'Tomorrow?' The Oracle sounded surprised. For a moment the wadi was silent, apart from the awful sounds of crunching from the cat. Finally she said quietly, 'Tomorrow, then. But tell no one! And on no account are you to come before Ra climbs a handspan into the sky.'

'What will happen if I do?'

The Oracle sighed. Her sigh sounded like a flute in a far-off courtyard, thought Narmer. 'Plagues of locusts. Boils filled with pus. Sandstorms. Now go. The oracle is finished.'

'May I bring the King? He will have questions too.'

There was no reply.

'Oracle?' called Narmer, then more loudly, 'Mighty Oracle?'

Silence.

'*Prraw,*' said the cat. There were a few shreds of lizard skin stuck to the fur around its mouth. Narmer looked away from the gruesome sight. He placed the other lizard on the ground and glanced hopefully at the rock again.

But the Oracle was silent.

CHAPTER 2

Did it really happen? thought Narmer, as he climbed out of the wadi again. Did I really speak to an oracle?

He glanced back into the wadi, but there was only red rock and shadows. Even the cat had vanished.

Shadows ... how much time had passed down in the wadi? He was going to be late. He broke into a run as he headed back along the cliff.

Down below on the River men fished from their small reed boats. Teams of naked workers repaired dykes, lifting baskets of mud up to the thick walls that protected the town and the palace, its painted colonnades gleaming in the sun.

Other dykes protected the orchards, with their tall date palms, sycamores, figs, grape vines and carob trees, tiny islands in the flood. From up here on the cliff Narmer could see the rounded shapes of the giant stones that marked out the boundaries of the fields, too. More workers planted papyrus, sedges and lotus in the shallows, all the while keeping an eye out for crocodiles lurking in the water.

A crocodile had already taken a small boy a few days ago. The bereft family had searched everywhere, but there had been no sign of the child, or the crocodile. As he ran Narmer shivered at the thought of the child's small body being pulled down into the dark water. The croc would be sleeping off its meal now, its long body the same colour as the mud.

Narmer glanced back down into the wadi. Maybe tomorrow the Oracle could tell him where the crocodile was, before it could kill again.

There was so much else he could have asked her!

Tomorrow, he thought. I will speak to her again tomorrow.

Her voice had been so lovely . . .

'*Hiss!*'

It was a line of brown geese, marching back home after a day puddling for half-submerged grass.

It was time he was home too.

He ran faster, half sliding down the hill towards the town. He'd already broken one rule: hunting without his guard. The King indulged his younger son, but he might not be so forgiving if Narmer turned up late and muddy for a feast. Especially not this afternoon, when there was a guest like the Trader in the palace.

Imagine a trader crossing the Endless Desert! Only the People of the Sand lived out there!

There were stories about a world beyond the Endless Desert, of course. That was where ebony came from, and cinnamon, and the more-than-precious myrrh, beloved of the gods for its rich scent and healing powers. What had the Oracle said that the Trader had brought with him? 'All the glories from beyond the furthest horizon!'

The Trader and his men had rested in the guesthouse today. This afternoon there was a feast, as befitted an honoured guest, and there would be another feast tomorrow. Only on the third day would business be discussed and the treasures unwrapped. And on the fourth day the Trader and his men would be gone, before the dew had risen from the ground. This was tradition too — no guest stayed for more than three days of hospitality.

One day I'll have to deal with traders by myself, thought Narmer. One day when I am king. I'll be the one who bargains our grain for ebony, or ivory from the south. The thought excited him.

He was near the town now. He splashed through the shallows up to the dyke, then ran along its top till he reached the gate in the high mud-brick walls, the first defence against the attacks of the People of the Sand from the desert, and the people of Yebu to the north.

Now that the water was falling Narmer could see where the flood had eaten chunks from the walls. They'll have to be repaired as soon as the water recedes a bit more, thought Narmer automatically.

That was the first question he'd ask the Oracle tomorrow, he decided: when would the People of the Sand attack again? And was there any way to arrange a truce with them, as his father had done by arranging a marriage between Narmer and the Princess of Yebu?

Now he was through the gate and into the main street, past Seto the flint knapper, past the barbers, still with a few customers to be shaved and oiled, past the bakers, their ovens cooling now in the late afternoon.

People stopped their work to stare at him as he ran past, to smile and bow. One of the bakers shuffled out, his body bent over as he held out a gift for Narmer. 'For you, o Golden One! May your beauty live a thousand years!' he cried, still bowing respectfully.

Narmer stopped and accepted the offering. It was a flat cake of date bread, sweet with wild honey and rich with sesame seeds.

Narmer bit into the soft crust and smiled. 'Thank you ... Fenotup, isn't it?'

The man's face lit up at having his name remembered. 'Yes, o Golden One. Blessings on you and your father and your father's house.'

'Blessings on your house too, Fenotup, and on your good bread and your oven.'

Narmer broke into a jog again, still munching on his bread. It was undignified, running and eating in full view of the people. But better than being late. And besides, he was the Golden One. Whatever the Golden One did must be right.

The palace stood higher than the rest of the town, on its own man-made hill, surrounded by high walls that were topped with sharp stones. Narmer climbed the steps and ducked through the low stone archway that led into the First Courtyard, with its long pool and fruit trees.

From here he could see the other courtyards through the colonnades: the women's quarters, where Father's women lived, and further along the servants' quarters, then on the other side the kitchen courtyard, with its lotus pool and fish ponds. Narmer glimpsed the flickers of a fire already lit for the afternoon meal, a platter of vegetables waiting to be peeled, giant pots of palm sap or date beer brewing in the

11

shade of the date palms, and women sitting in the shade of acacia and sycamore trees, grinding the wheat and barley for tomorrow's bread.

The guest quarters were in their own walled area beyond the main palace, though guests were attended by the palace servants. Guests were strangers, so it was safer not to admit them into the heart of the palace itself.

Narmer's rooms were near the King's. He had moved there from the women's quarters when he was six. His brother Hawk's rooms were further away, fine rooms, as befitted a son of King Scorpion. But neither as grand nor as near the King as Narmer's.

He could hear old Seknut's cough as she approached while he was washing his face and arms in the basin in the corner of his private courtyard. Seknut had been his mother's nurse, then his nurse after his mother died when he was born. Sometimes Narmer wondered what it would be like to have a mother. But even though Seknut was a servant, not even able to touch her royal charge these days without permission, Narmer was sure that no one else could have cared for him so devotedly.

These days Seknut's back was bent, her teeth were worn to stumps, and she had the sand cough badly. But she still kept a sharp eye on everything, from his tooth cleaning to the contents of his chamber pot.

Narmer grinned at her affectionately as she draped his clean kilt over the big wooden chest in the corner of the room. 'I know. I'm late.'

Seknut gave a shadow of a bow, then sat on the edge of the bed and peered at him short-sightedly. It was forbidden to sit without permission in the presence of the royal family. But no one had ever had the courage to remind her.

'Look at you! Barefoot like a baker's boy! Where were you?' Other servants would have bowed to the ground, called him Prince or Golden One. But it was unrealistic to expect someone who had wiped your bum as a baby to do all that.

'Hunting.'

'Your royal father sent for you. I had to tell him I didn't know where you were.' Seknut sounded as though the crime of not telling her were far greater than that of disappointing a king.

Narmer grinned again. 'I bet he guessed where I'd gone. He used to slip off hunting too when he was my age.'

'Your feet are dirty. It's not seemly for a prince to be seen with bare feet.'

'My sandals slip on the rock.' Narmer rubbed the dust off his chest with a damp cloth, then began to wash his feet as well.

'You should bathe properly.'

'No time.'

Seknut coughed again. She watched as Narmer undid his everyday kilt and wrapped the clean one about his waist. It was his best, made of finely woven linen bleached white by the sun, with a thin band of red about the hem. Then he pulled on his jewellery: a gold armlet and an antelope-bone necklace with a polished amulet.

Seknut gave a small approving smile, the same one she'd given all those years ago when he managed to use his pot instead of mess the floor.

'What have you found out about the Trader?' demanded Narmer. Seknut heard everything that happened in the palace. No servant would dare keep a secret from Seknut.

'His men are polite, and they know how to wash and not throw their bones on the floor.' She wrinkled her nose. 'But that animal of theirs smells.'

'What animal?' Narmer dragged a comb through his long hair.

'They have a —' She broke off as the sound of a flute filtered through the colonnades. The feast had begun. 'Hurry!' she urged. 'Your royal father will be annoyed.'

'Do I look all right?'

Seknut inspected him. 'You'll do.' Other people heaped praised on the Golden One, but this was as close to a compliment as Seknut ever came.

Narmer patted her hand. 'I'll save you a hunk of hippopotamus from the feast.'

Seknut's eyes almost vanished into her wrinkles as she glared at him. 'And how would my old gums eat hippopotamus? Nasty tough meat it is.'

'Every hippo we eat is one less in the fields.' Hippopotamuses were the worst pests of the flood season, pushing their way through the carefully built dykes so that water flooded into the orchards and swamped the trees.

'The cook has made mutton bread,' said Seknut, trying to sound casual. Sheep's meat was reserved for the King and his family and honoured guests. But Narmer knew Seknut loved the tiny pastries filled with minced meat, fruit and the soft fat from sheep's tails.

'I'll save you some,' he called as he ran out the door.

CHAPTER 3

Narmer slowed down as he reached the end of the colonnade that led to Royal Courtyard. It wouldn't do to gallop in like an ox stung by bees. He glanced through the painted pillars. His father and brother were already seated under the sycamore and carob trees by the lotus pool.

That other man must be the Trader, thought Narmer. He felt a flash of disappointment. The Trader looked just like anybody else. He was older than Narmer had expected. His beard was grey and trimmed square as a house brick. His head was almost bald, and his face was wrinkled like a brown fig left to dry in the sun. A fourth person sat there too, his face hidden by a scarf.

Narmer walked sedately through the archway of flaming bougainvillea flowers and bowed his face to the tiles respectfully. 'Father.'

'My son.' The King waved a hand to the stool beside him. During feasts only the King sat on a throne, and only his heir sat on a stool. The others sat on cushions, except for the flute player in the shadows, his music no louder than the tinkle of the fountain, who sat cross-legged on a woven mat.

Narmer sat down and nodded at his brother, who smiled back pleasantly. Hawk was always pleasant to his brother. Sometimes — especially when he was younger — Narmer had wished his brother would be ... different. Laugh with him, play ball with him, even argue with him like other brothers he sometimes saw in the streets of Thinis, quarrelling then making up, then squabbling again, even their arguments showing how close they were.

But Hawk stayed distant. Perhaps, thought Narmer, it was part of being royal.

Hawk was in his early twenties, almost twice Narmer's age. He was tall and good-looking enough, Narmer had always thought, apart from his eyes, which bulged like a frog's, and his skin, which was pitted from the pimples he'd had when he was younger.

Narmer had sometimes wondered if Hawk would have been his father's heir if only he had been as handsome as Narmer. Would the people have loved Hawk more if his skin had been smooth and golden?

Narmer knew that if he had been in Hawk's position he would have found it hard to accept the King's decision. But the King represented the gods. Whatever the King said *had* to be right. And Hawk had never shown that he felt the King's choice was anything but wise. When Narmer was king Hawk would make the perfect vizier, supporting his brother's decisions for the good of the land.

Tonight Hawk was the perfect prince. He had dressed with far more care than Narmer. He had even shaved, and had plucked the hairs from his hands and arms.

Narmer forgot about his brother, and glanced at the Trader instead. Had someone as well dressed as this really come through the Endless Desert? It was hard to believe that there was anything of value beyond the River.

The Trader gazed back at him thoughtfully. Unlike the bare-chested locals, the Trader wore a tunic that covered his chest and arms and fell almost to his ankles. His only ornament was the garland of poppies and lotus flowers around his shoulders that the palace women had made for the guest of honour at the feast.

The Trader's companion wore the concealing tunic too, as well as a headdress, and the scarf that hid his mouth and nose. Only his eyes showed, and his hands and feet. His hands were small and slender. Young hands, thought Narmer.

He sniffed. The companion smelt ... strange. A scent of spices, and an almost familiar animal smell too. Was there something odd about the boy's feet as well? Yes — one was scarred so badly that half the ankle looked eaten away. Narmer wondered how the young man had managed to walk through the desert.

Suddenly he realised he'd been staring. He forced his gaze away from the strangers and smiled at his father instead.

'You're late,' said the King affectionately, smiling back at his son. The King wore his usual starched kilt, and the gold belt with the bull's tail hanging from it: the symbol of his power. There was gold at his wrists and on his sandals too.

'I'm sorry, Your Majesty. I was ...' Narmer hesitated. He wanted to tell the King about his adventure with the Oracle to excuse his lateness — and also to get the King's advice on what questions to ask tomorrow. But the Oracle was too important for dinner conversation. Besides, it was . . . private.

'I was hunting,' he said instead.

The King frowned. 'By yourself?'

'Yes, Your Majesty.'

'How many times have I told you —'

'How you ran to the hills when you were my age? Many times!' said Narmer, grinning up at his father. 'And of course there was the time you hunted that hippopotamus all by yourself . . .'

The King broke into laughter. 'You see how he rules me?' he asked the Trader proudly. 'Let us hope he rules the country with as much zeal and success.'

The Trader's expression didn't change. He doesn't understand, Narmer realised. He's like the People of the Sand. He doesn't know our speech.

'If you'll permit, great King?' The voice behind the scarf was soft and low-pitched. There was an almost-accent too, a curious lilt to the words.

He's young, thought Narmer, no older than I am, perhaps. Perhaps the young man covered his mouth so it would seem that the master said the words, not the servant.

The King nodded. The young man began to translate for his master, so softly and quickly that it was hard to make out the words.

The Trader's face broke into a grin. He said something to the Translator.

'My master says he would like to hear the tale of the king who single-handedly caught a hippopotamus, o great King of all magnificence,' translated the young man quietly.

The King laughed as he gestured to the servants to bring in the food. 'I was only a prince back then, Narmer's age, a year older perhaps. There was a high flood that year, and ...'

Narmer hardly listened. He had heard the story many times, from both Seknut and the King. Instead, he looked at the food as the servants began to bring in the platters. He was hungry, despite the snack that the baker had given him. The King and his family always ate well, but tonight would be special, to honour their guest.

There was no hippopotamus, as Narmer had promised Seknut. But there were hunks of roast mutton, deliciously greasy, as well as the mutton pastries that Seknut had craved. There were roast reed birds stuffed with figs, grilled catfish, date bread, honey bread, fig bread, goose eggs baked till they were hard and served with yoghurt sauce, beans baked in a pot with wild honey and herbs, the first of the season's papyrus stems, steamed till they were soft, a dish of leeks and celery, and barley beer or bright red pomegranate juice to drink.

The servants knelt before the King, then rose to offer the food to each person: first the King, then Narmer, then the Trader, then Prince Hawk, and finally the Trader's companion. But the young man ate little, lifting the food up under his scarf as he nibbled at shreds of meat or papyrus stem.

Finally platters of jujubes, dried grapes, and stuffed figs and dates were left on the ground for everyone to help themselves, with the King's favourite dishes placed on a table by his throne.

The King finished his story and the guests murmured appreciatively. The King picked up a cluster of raisins and chewed one pensively. 'Perhaps,' he said to the Translator, 'your master might have a story of his own. We would be honoured to hear something of his travels.'

The Translator turned to his master. Once again the words were almost too soft and rapid to follow.

The Trader looked thoughtful again. He glanced up at Narmer, as though coming to a decision. Then he began to speak, and the Translator's low voice echoed his words.

'O great King, ruler of the most magnificent town on the most glorious of rivers, my master will tell you of his first voyage, when he was no older than Prince Narmer — may your son have peace and plenty for many years.'

The Translator bowed his head respectfully to Narmer. His husky voice continued. 'My master travelled with his grandfather and thirty men. But halfway across the sea their ship was hit by a storm.'

'You can count?' asked Narmer. Few people could count further than their fingers. It was hard to believe that anyone beyond the River could be so skilled.

He could almost hear the smile in the young man's voice. 'Of course, o glorious Prince. What use is a humble trader's servant who can't count?'

'But how can a boat carry thirty men?' cried Narmer.

'You are discourteous, my son,' rebuked the King.

'I'm sorry, Father. But —'

'There are ships in other lands that are much larger than your fishing boats,' said the Translator. 'But this is my master's story . . .

'The waves leapt like goats, and were as high as hills. For three days the ship was tossed like wheat at the threshing.

But on the fourth night the wind vanished. When the crew woke the sea was as flat as unleavened bread. And there was an island in front of them.

'It was a bare island, just two hills like skulls, side by side. No trees. No sand. Just rock down to the shore.

'But that wasn't the strangest thing. From the island came the most glorious voice my master had ever heard.

'It was a woman, singing. Even now, after all his years, my master says he has never heard a voice like it.'

The Trader interrupted, his voice suddenly harsh. Once again his gaze seemed focused on Narmer alone.

'Or wanted to,' the boy translated quietly.

The Trader began to speak again. The Translator took up the tale, talking easily, as though he could both listen and translate at the same time. Or perhaps, thought Narmer, he had heard this story so many times before that he knew it by heart.

'The shore was too rocky for the ship to beach safely. But there was a smaller boat on board, about the size of the reed boats on your river here. Every man on board longed to be first ashore, to find the woman who sang so sweetly. But the boat could only carry two men at a time.

'So the Captain went first, with a sailor to paddle. They leapt onto the rocks, pulled up the canoe and ran between the hills.

'And my master waited, and so did everyone else on board.

'But the Captain didn't return. And still the song came from the island, the sweetest voice it was possible to hear.

'One of the sailors could swim, so my master's grandfather sent him to bring the boat back. Then my master's

21

grandfather set out with another sailor. But before he left he took his grandson, my master, aside.

'"If I do not return, do not look for me," he said. "I entrust the ship, her cargo and the men to you. Sail away. Do not look back and never look for me again."

'"Why, Grandfather?" my master cried.

'But his grandfather wouldn't answer.

'My master watched them paddle across the water, until they too pulled up at the rocks and went ashore, then vanished between the hills.

'The shadows grew longer and still no one came back. The voice sang as sweetly as ever. Night fell, and the voice died away. But still no one came down to the boat at the shore.

'No one on board slept that night. The sailors were waiting for the voice to sing again. And my master was waiting for his grandfather.

'Dawn rose, pink and clear. And as the sun climbed above the waves the voice began to sing again.

'My master hesitated till the sun was at its height. He knew he should obey his grandfather's command. But he also knew that if he left his grandfather stranded on the island, he could never forgive himself.

'So he begged the sailor to swim to the island again. And when the boat was brought back my master and the sailor began to paddle across to the island.

'Closer and closer they came ... The voice grew louder, and sweeter too. They pulled the boat up onto the rocks.

'My master said, "Wait! We must go carefully. You wait here and —"

'But the sailor had already gone. Like the others, he was mesmerised by the voice and had vanished into the gully between the hills.'

The Trader stopped, to drink from his mug. The Translator stopped politely too, though Narmer was sure the young man could have finished the story by himself.

The Trader cleared his throat. He looked thoughtfully at Narmer for a moment, then began again.

'The others had all disappeared between the rocks. So my master crept up the hill instead, sneaked over the summit on his belly and looked down.

'There was a clearing between the hills, hidden from the sea. A woman sat on one of the rocks. All my master could see was her hair, long and black and shining like a river in full flood. For a moment she seemed as beautiful as her voice.

'And then she turned, so he could glimpse her face. It looked young. Her features were lovely, except for her eyes, as cold as ashes. Her mouth was black, and so were her teeth and hands.

'And the black was ... blood,' said the Translator simply. 'Dried blood. There was a blowpipe beside her, with thorns that might have been poison darts. And there, tied to stakes, were the Captain, the two sailors and my master's grandfather, with blood draining from wounds in their necks into stone cups below.'

Narmer felt his skin crawl, as if ants were creeping over him. 'But ... but what ...' he began.

'She was an afreet,' said the Translator in his low voice. 'In the desert they lure a man out into the endless dry to

23

send him mad. At sea they lure men from their ships and then they feast on them.

'But what was worse — so much worse — was that my master's grandfather saw my master up on the cliff as the blood dripped from his veins. But he couldn't move.

'My master tried to read the expression in his eyes. Was he calling for rescue, or to be left to die so his grandson might be safe?

'It didn't matter. My master flung himself down the cliff onto the afreet. It was obvious she didn't expect anything of the kind as his knife went into her back. She turned, her eyes wide, and my master saw that her teeth were crusted with the skin of men. Her breath smelt worse than a hundred privies, for privies do not smell of death.

'"How did you resist me?" she whispered.

'"My manhood was stolen from me years ago," said my master. "But it seems that the thieves have unknowingly given me my life."'

'She smiled at that. Even though the knife was lodged in her back she could still smile.

'"I have sung here for a thousand years," she said. "An afreet cannot die of old age, not while she drinks the blood of living men. A thousand years of blood and loneliness ... You have given me the gift of death. So I will give you a gift as well."

'Her voice was just a whisper now. "Continue travelling," she said, "and this I promise. A dying promise cannot lie. One day as you travel you will find your son and daughter."

'And then she gave a gurgle, blood flowed from her mouth and she was dead.

'My master ran to his grandfather. But his eyes were sightless as they stared into the sky.

'So my master closed them. He buried his grandfather in the dirt of the island, and the others too. But he left the afreet for the crows.

'Then he returned to the ship. And he has travelled ever since.'

The Trader no longer looked at his audience. His gaze was fixed on the lotus pool, or perhaps somewhere very far away.

'But I don't understand,' objected Narmer. 'What did your master mean when he said his manhood was stolen from him? Why were the other men trapped while he escaped?'

'Because my master can never be lured by the song of a woman,' said the Translator softly.

'Why not?' cried Narmer.

Hawk gave a small cough from his cushion on the other side of the courtyard. 'Because he is a eunuch,' he said pleasantly, his frog eyes narrowing as he smiled. 'Isn't that so?'

'But he has a beard!' Eunuchs never grew whiskers, just as they were unable to have children.

The Translator said something to the Trader. The Trader smiled and met Narmer's eyes once again. He reached behind his ears and suddenly his beard fell into his lap.

The Trader said something to the Translator, still with his eyes on Narmer.

'My master says that not everything is as it seems, Prince Narmer,' the young man translated.

'My master was captured in a rebel raid back in his homeland, Sumer, when he was not much more than a toddler. His father led a party of soldiers to bring him back. But by then his manhood had been cut away.'

'But ...' Narmer tried to think. 'But how can he ever have a son and daughter?'

'I am sorry, so sorry, great Prince. I cannot tell you. My master himself doesn't know.' The Translator's voice was low, as though he shared his master's sadness. But there was something more, thought Narmer suddenly. It was almost as though in his sorrow the Translator spoke in another voice. 'He believes that one day, nevertheless, he will find his son and daughter. A dying promise never lies, even from an afreet. That is why he keeps on travelling. He knows that one day he will find them.'

The Translator's voice was back to normal. I was imagining things, thought Narmer. A servant glided from the shadows at a gesture from the King and filled their mugs again. Narmer sipped and let the conversation wash over him.

It was nearly too much to take in. It had almost seemed as though the Trader were telling the story just to him. As though there were a message for him alone.

But how could there be? Narmer wasn't a trader. Nor was he hunting for the son and daughter he had never had.

He glanced at the Trader. The man still seemed lost in thought. And the Translator's face was hidden. But his brother gazed at him across the courtyard. In the growing shadows Hawk's face seemed almost amused.

CHAPTER 4

The next day Narmer woke before dawn. He needed to leave before his father's guards saw him and tried to accompany him.

A pang of guilt went through him. One day's hunting was excusable. But two days in a row, when the dykes needed checking now that the floods were going down ...

Yet he *had* to see the Oracle. Surely when he told his father he'd understand. There was so much the Oracle could tell him that would help Thinis.

He peered out of his room. No, no one about, not even the early sweepers in the royal courtyard. Every floor and street in Thinis had to be swept each morning, or the sand soon formed small dunes against the walls. Even during the floods the dust blew in from the hills, and the sand from the deserts beyond.

Narmer slipped out through the courtyard, then under the archway.

'Where are you off to?' A soft voice came from the shadows under the colonnades.

Narmer turned. It was Hawk. He leant against the walls of the palace, regarding Narmer with his usual small smile.

'Hunting.' Narmer held up his spears and slingshot, and a small bundle of food.

'Off to catch a hippopotamus on your own, like our celebrated father?'

'Nothing so grand,' said Narmer. 'Maybe a few pigeons. A fox or gazelle if I'm lucky.'

'What a pity,' said Hawk gently. 'I'm sure a hippo would impress our father. It would be a compliment to have a son who caught a hippo, just like him.'

Narmer grinned. 'Maybe one day. See you this afternoon.'

'Have fun, little brother.' Hawk lifted a hand in farewell. His hands were always smooth, the hairs plucked with tweezers, the nails buffed with wax.

Narmer broke into a jog as soon as he'd left the palace, acknowledging the bows and greetings of other early-rising people as he passed. The air was rich with the smells of baking bread and lotus-root cakes, and bubbling spiced-bean stews.

He hurried along the dyke again, then up into the hills. He could see women washing down below, beating their clothes by the water's edge.

Since yesterday the floods had retreated another cubit, leaving their black silt behind. The valley smelt of flood, and the promise of crops to come. Narmer smiled. The women wouldn't get their clothes very clean, no matter how much laundry paste of fat and wood ash they used. But he supposed it was too long to wait till the water ran clear again, and green grass and herbs and wild lettuce sprang up from the mud.

The smell of flood vanished once he reached the cliff, and the scent of the desert filled his nostrils instead. In front of him were hot rock and hotter sand stretching to the horizon, and the endless dry of the lands beyond the River.

No wonder the People of the Sand try to invade our lands, thought Narmer. How could anyone survive out there?

He continued along the ridge. A lizard poked its flat head up from behind a rock. Narmer felt for one of the stones in his pouch and fitted it into his sling.

Wham! The smooth rock hit the animal straight in the head. It fell to the ground, stunned. Narmer ran over to it and broke its neck swiftly, before it could wake up, then hung its carcass from his belt.

He began to jog again. Soon the Oracle's wadi was below him ...

All at once he remembered that the Oracle had ordered him not to come before noon. He glanced above him. Ra's golden chariot hovered just above the hills. He was early.

Would she be angry?

He gazed down into the wadi. There was no sign of the wildcat today.

Then suddenly there it was, slinking through a crevice in the rock. He hadn't noticed the crevice among the shadows yesterday.

The giant cat stared up at him. '*Mrraw?*'

It lay down on the rock again. Its golden eyes gazed at Narmer as he half climbed, half slid down the cliff.

Narmer chose a spot well away from the watchful cat, then bowed, his face to the ground. 'Mighty Oracle?'

'Yes?' Somehow the Oracle sounded short of breath, almost as if she had been running. He must be imagining it, he thought. Oracles didn't run; they were just *there*. 'I told you not to seek me before noon,' she added. Despite the edge in her voice, it was as lovely as it had been the day before.

'I wanted to see you,' said Narmer simply.

There was a pause. 'You can't *see* an oracle.' And strangely there was a hint of bitterness in the words. 'You can only *hear* her.'

'Hear you then, o mighty Oracle,' said Narmer quickly. 'Ask you questions.'

'Proceed, then.'

'When will the People of the Sand attack again?'

'That's easy. You should know the answer yourself.'

Narmer considered. 'After the next harvest,' he said slowly.

'Of course. Isn't that when they've attacked in the past? When the granaries are full and desert bellies empty. Next question.'

'What should I do when I am king?'

'Your best, of course.' The Oracle laughed as Narmer frowned. 'That wasn't the answer you wanted, was it? All right. Build your walls higher. Train your men in fighting. Don't just wait for an attack to teach them how to wield a spear or a club. There's been a drought to the east and west. More tribes are moving towards the River. There's little food in the desert, and lots of barley and wheat in your granaries. Is that all you want to ask?'

'One more question ...' Narmer took a deep breath. 'If you had a body and not just a voice, what would you look like?'

There was another pause. 'I would be tall,' said the Oracle softly. 'With skin the colour of the moonlit sand. And I would be perfect. Is that the end of your questions?'

'I think so, o Oracle. For today.'

Narmer was still trying to take it all in. Tribes moving from the desert to Thinis. He'd have to tell his father. They'd have to plan ...

The voice spoke again. 'There will be no other day. Ask what you want now.'

Narmer's eyes opened wide in shock. 'Why? I'll have other questions on other days!'

'Because that's the way it is,' said the Oracle shortly.

'But I *have* to speak to you again!' cried Narmer.

'What question is so difficult that you have to ask it tomorrow, not today?'

'I — I just want to talk to you!' It was true, he realised. Being a prince could be lonely. But here was someone — some*thing* — he could talk to. Who understood more than just the types of fish in the nets and what sort of bread was for dinner.

More silence. 'I'm sorry, so sorry,' said the voice softly. 'I can't come again. I wish I could. So sorry ...'

Narmer frowned. For a moment the voice had been almost familiar. As though in her sorrow the Oracle had spoken without thinking, using a different voice from the one she had used before ...

I can't come again, she had said. But oracles didn't have bodies. How could the Oracle *come again*? And that phrase,

31

sorry, so sorry. Where had he heard it before? With that same almost-accent?

'*Mrrrr?*' said the cat into the silence. It sat up again, sending a waft of cat scent across the gully.

The scent of cat. And the musky, animal scent the night before, under the scent of spices.

'I know who you are,' said Narmer quietly.

'What do you mean?' The Oracle's old voice was back again, without the hint of accent. 'I'm an oracle.'

'No, you're not. You're a young man, like me. You're the Trader's translator.'

'I'm not!'

'You are. There's a crevice in the rock. I didn't see it among the shadows yesterday. That's where you're hiding.' Narmer tried to keep the anger from his voice. 'Come on. Come out where I can see you.'

'Why?'

'Why do you think?' said Narmer bitterly. 'So I can give you the beating you deserve. Pretending to be an oracle! Pretending to have a girl's voice!'

'I didn't pretend! I'm not a boy.'

'Are you still claiming you're an oracle?'

'No. I'm not an oracle. I'm a girl.'

CHAPTER 5

The cat stood up, waving its huge tail from side to side. Its golden eyes flashed at Narmer as though he were a desert mouse who might dare to resist becoming breakfast.

Narmer took a step back. 'What's wrong with it?' he called to the unseen watcher in the crevice. 'Is it going to attack me?' He lifted his spear.

'She knows you're angry with me,' said the girl's voice coolly. 'Throw her the lizard on your belt.'

'Will that stop her?'

He could almost hear the shrug. 'Maybe.'

Narmer untied the bit of dried gut that held the lizard and threw the animal to the cat. She caught it in her teeth before it hit the ground. She stopped for a moment, as though considering whether to accept it, then padded back to her rock and ripped open its belly with her teeth.

Narmer let out the breath he didn't know he was holding. He wasn't sure he would have had time to hurl his spear if she had leapt.

'Thank you,' he said to the blank cliff face. 'But I still want to see you.'

Another pause. 'To thrash me?'

'No, I don't beat girls. I want an explanation.'

'I wanted to talk to you, that's all.'

'Why not talk to me at the palace? Or won't your master let you?'

'What? Oh, no. My master is very good to me.'

'Then why? Why trick me like that?'

Something moved behind the rock face. Narmer heard the sound of feet limping across the sand.

For a moment the young man of the night before stood there in the shadows of the crevice. The same long robe, the same scarf across the face. And then the scarf was lowered.

Narmer gasped.

'Yes,' said the girl bitterly. 'Now you know why I hide behind a scarf and rock, Prince Narmer. Now you know.'

They sat in the sunlight, a little away from the cat as she tore at the lizard.

Narmer cast another look at the girl. He was trying not to stare, but it was difficult. Her face was scarred all down one side, the skin as red and rippled as a pool in the rock. Her lip twisted in an eternal half smile.

Narmer said nothing. There was nothing he could think to say.

'My name is Nithotep,' said the girl at last. She sat with her face averted, trying to hide the scarred side of her face. 'My master calls me Nitho.'

'Where are you from?'

'From a land called Ka'naan — or so my master says. I don't remember. He found me out in the desert when he was trading there. I'd been badly burnt. My face, my legs, my arm too, as though I had fallen in the fire. But he said I was still crawling, trying to get home. I was two years old, perhaps. No more.

'My master knows medicine. There are experts in his land who have taught him about healing, and he's learnt even more as he's travelled. He tended my burns. He tried to find my parents, but no one claimed me.'

Narmer stayed silent. He could imagine that the parents of a child as badly hurt as that might not want to have her back. Babies who were badly formed, or even too small, were exposed on the rocks for the jackals to eat. An older child who was scarred, perhaps crippled, would be no use at all. Especially a girl. What man would take a crippled girl to marry?

'So my master kept me,' said Nitho quietly. 'He forced me to move my arms and legs when the scars would have pulled tight and twisted my limbs. He cared for me.'

'Why?' Narmer bluntly. A trader could buy all the girls he wanted — beautiful ones, not scarred ones like Nitho.

'Because I had survived,' said Nitho softly. 'Just like he had when he was captured and hurt as a child. He told me that a child who had fought as I had would become an adult who could survive as well. One whom he would be honoured to travel with.'

'My nurse was a slave from along your River, captured and sold by the People of the Sand. That's how I can speak your language. My master had me taught many other languages as we travelled. He is the wisest man I know, but even a wise man can't know everything, and he has no ear for other tongues. So I became his translator.'

'Why do you dress as a man?'

Nitho shrugged. 'There are places where it isn't safe to be a girl. I'm used to putting on a boy's voice. Like this.' Suddenly her voice was gruff again. 'But mostly because ...' She spoke in her own voice again. 'Who wants to look at a face like mine?'

'So you wear the scarf all the time?'

'Not when we're travelling. My master says the first time you see a girl with a scar like mine you say, "Look at the scar." The second time you say, "There is Nitho with the scar." But the third time you say, "There is Nitho." Those who know me don't see my scar any more.' She hesitated a moment then added, 'But they don't see beauty either.'

'That was what your master meant last night when he told the story,' said Narmer slowly. 'He was saying that appearances can be deceptive.'

'Yes. It's one of his favourites. I think he tells it to make me feel better. A beautiful voice tells you nothing about the person behind it. And an ugly face ...' She shrugged again. 'Well, maybe the person behind that isn't as bad as she looks either.'

For the first time Nitho looked straight at him. 'But this was the only chance I'd ever have of talking to someone like you. Someone who would speak to me without revulsion. I was taking Bast out for a walk — she was making the people in the guesthouse nervous, and —'

'Bast?'

Nitho nodded at the wildcat. 'I raised her from a kitten. One of her legs had been almost torn off by jackals. But my master showed me how to sew up the wound, to make her whole. Anyway, I was taking her for a walk and I saw you here. I hid and ... well, you know the rest.'

Narmer said nothing.

'No more questions?' asked Nitho, smiling slightly.

Narmer shook his head. He could think of nothing else to say.

This girl had fooled him completely. She had learnt enough about Thinis in one day to answer all his questions. He didn't wonder that her master kept her with him.

She had even made him believe that she was beautiful ...

'What will you do now?' he asked at last.

She shrugged. 'Go back to the guesthouse.'

'No, I mean when you and your master leave here.'

'We'll head back the way we came. Across the desert, then across the sea towards my master's homeland, Sumer. And after that ... who knows?'

Narmer tried to imagine it. Always travelling, never with your own people, not even speaking your own language. 'Will you ever come back here?'

Nitho shook her head. 'I don't think so. We only came this time because an oracle told my master that he would find great fortune here.' She smiled briefly. The scar on her face twisted even more. 'That's where I got the idea to pretend to be an oracle. But no matter what the Oracle said, I don't think Thinis will have riches enough to make it worth crossing the desert again.'

'I see,' said Narmer slowly.

'*Would* you have talked to me, Prince Narmer, if I'd met you in the palace?' Nitho asked suddenly. 'Tell me honestly.'

Narmer was silent for a moment. 'Honestly? I would have been polite to a guest,' he said at last. 'But no. We wouldn't have talked for long.'

Nitho stood up. 'Then there is no need for us to talk now. I will see you tonight, Prince Narmer, and tomorrow when we trade, but I'll be my master's voice then, not my own. Goodbye. We won't speak again.' She began to limp away.

Bast looked up. She grabbed the remains of the lizard in her jaws and padded after Nitho. She didn't even look back at Narmer.

'No! Stop!' cried Narmer. He couldn't bear to see them go like that.

But Nitho didn't hesitate. A few seconds later she and Bast were gone.

CHAPTER 6

Narmer met his father's guards as he came along the ridge towards home. For a moment he wondered if scouts from the People of the Sand had been spotted. Then he realised the guards were looking for *him*.

The men bowed. 'Your royal father is angry, o great Prince,' said the leader.

'I am sorry to have angered him,' said Narmer shortly. His mind was still filled with what had happened. How could Nitho have tricked him like that? Why hadn't he realised before? 'Have you come to escort me on my hunt?'

'No, Prince.' The guard looked embarrassed. 'We have come to take you back to the palace.'

Narmer stared at the man. How dare they take him back, like a child who had been left to feed the fire but had gone out to play! No one had ever treated him like that before.

But there was no use complaining to the guards. They were only following the King's orders. And no one questioned the King — not even his son.

The small group marched back to the palace in silence. Narmer had never felt less like speaking in his life, and out of respect that meant none of the men could speak either.

'Where is the King?' asked Narmer as they approached the town walls. 'In the Royal Courtyard? Out inspecting the dykes? I'll go to him at once.'

'The King said that you were to go to your rooms,' said the guard awkwardly.

Narmer flushed. To be sent to his rooms, like a child! But he simply nodded. He walked along the colonnades to his rooms, trying to keep his dignity.

And there he stayed.

No one came to him all afternoon. Finally he could hear music and voices, and smell the smoke from roasting meat. The Trader's second feast must have begun.

But even old Seknut didn't appear, to scold him into washing and make sure he wore his best. No one brought him food either.

He could have called a servant to bring him bread, at least. But he wouldn't. This was the King's punishment. He would bear it as befitted a prince, in dignity and silence.

Finally the sounds from the courtyard died away. The palace was quiet. Even the palace ferrets had stopped scurrying after mice.

But he couldn't sleep. It was partly hunger, but it was more than that. His brain kept buzzing like a wild beehive.

Had Nitho wondered why he wasn't at the banquet? Had his father explained that it was a punishment? Or did she think he was avoiding her? He wasn't sure which was worse.

For the first time he began to understand what it must be like for a girl with a scarred face and crippled limbs. What use was a girl who would never be married?

But she *was* useful, he realised. She was a translator. Narmer spoke no other language himself, but he had some idea of how difficult it must be to speak another's tongue. And not just one. She had said that she spoke many ...

He was still angry with her. He was still embarrassed, especially after his punishment.

But for some reason he still wanted to see her again ...

Finally he slept.

He still hadn't decided what to tell his father when Seknut came to take him to the King the next morning. How could he explain that Nitho had warned him about the People of the Sand without revealing how she had deceived him?

No, it would be best to wait till the Trader had left. Then he could pretend that it had been the Trader who had spoken to him, not the Trader's servant.

Seknut had brought him barley bread studded with raisins, and a glass of sour milk and honey. With her was a servant carrying fresh water for Narmer to wash in and a clean linen kilt, a good one.

'Hurry,' Seknut said, muffling her cough behind her hand.

Narmer gulped down the bread. 'Is he still angry?'

Seknut shrugged. 'He is the King. He doesn't tell me his thoughts.'

Narmer snorted. Seknut knew everything. Or did she? he wondered.

He drank the milk quickly, changed, then slipped his jewellery on as well, as though he were dressing for a feast.

For the first time since he had met the Oracle he suddenly remembered that soon there would be an even greater feast, for his bride. But now the thought brought no excitement. It seemed to belong to another world.

When Narmer entered the Royal Courtyard the King was seated on his ceremonial chair, with Hawk on a cushion at his feet. Hawk gave his brother an almost imperceptible smile, as though to say, *I'm on your side*.

Narmer didn't dare smile back, but was grateful nonetheless.

'Well, my son?' said the King.

Narmer knelt low, his face against the tiles, as though he were a servant, not a prince. 'I'm sorry, Father.'

'Are you? You may get up,' the King added impatiently.

Narmer got to his feet and shook his head. 'I am sorry to have angered you, Father. It's just that ... I need to be alone sometimes. It's hard to think, sometimes, with others always around you.'

'But that's what happens when you're king. Do you think there aren't times when I too long to be alone in the hills?'

'I ... I never thought,' stammered Narmer.

The King said nothing for a moment. Then he nodded to Hawk. 'Leave us,' he said shortly.

Hawk's face stayed expressionless as he made a deep bow to the King, then a smaller bow to Narmer. He backed out of the room, politely keeping his face towards his father.

The King gazed at Narmer before speaking. 'Do you know what it is to be king, Narmer?' he asked at last.

'Of course,' said Narmer, surprised.

'Do you really? The king is the bridge between men and the gods. That is why men bow to us. Not because we are greater than they are. But because we *have* to be greater than they are to do our duty. If it is ever easy to be a king, then you know you have failed.'

'I think I see.'

'I hope so. There is never a moment when a king can say, "I want to do this." A king can only say, "This is what I need to do for my country."

'I didn't make you my heir because you are my beloved son. I chose you because when I looked at you, I saw a king. Was I wrong, my son?'

'No, Father,' said Narmer quietly.

'Good. But there is another reason why I punished you. I was worried,' added the King softly. 'That is why I was angry. Sometimes it is impossible not to feel as a father, even as you do your duty as a king. I want you safe.'

'But I can take care of myself! Father, don't forbid me to go out without guards. Just sometimes ...'

His father shook his head. 'I want your promise,' he said. 'No more hunting by yourself. A king can risk himself in battle, for his people. But not just because he wants a day's sport.'

'I ... I promise,' said Narmer.

'Good. Now, sit down. The Trader has his wares to show us.'

CHAPTER 7

The King clapped his hands and servants hurried in with refreshments: cups of date beer and the precious milk that only the royal family and their guests were allowed to drink; chickpea cakes spiced with cumin and onions; and fresh radishes and bread, with plates of spiced lotus seed to dip them into.

Hawk returned and cast a sharp look at Narmer, then sat down on his usual cushion by the King.

Narmer seated himself on his stool as the Trader's porters carried bales wrapped in goatskin past the lotus pool. They were enormous men, with even darker skin than the Trader, and black curly hair. One had what looked like a puckered spear scar just below his shoulder. Another's eye was white and sightless.

Narmer tried not to stare at them. He had seen a few black-skinned people before, travelling with the People of the Sand, but none lived near the town of Thinis.

Now the Trader appeared, striding across the courtyard as though he were crossing the desert. Nitho limped behind him, her thick robes rustling and the scarf again obscuring her hair and face.

The Trader bowed.

'My master says, "Greetings, o great King Scorpion, o noble Prince Narmer and Prince Hawk."' Nitho was using her young man's voice again, Narmer noticed, deliberately lower and gruffer. 'May your shadows never grow less. Shall we begin?'

The King nodded.

The porters spread a fine linen cloth across the tiled floor of the courtyard. Narmer's eyes grew wide as one by one the bales were unwrapped.

Panther skins, black as night and soft as night air.

Slabs of smooth black ebony wood, the hardest, densest, richest wood in the world.

Cups of ivory carved as thin as eggshells, with birds and lions leaping on their sides.

A small wooden chest, with strange curls of what looked like bark inside.

'Smell them,' said Nitho softly.

Narmer picked up one of the curls. It was the richest, sweetest scent he had ever known.

'Cinnamon,' explained Nitho.

Her long slim fingers opened another chest. Narmer looked inside.

This one contained small brown balls, with another scent, deeper, more powerful.

The King looked at the Trader, eyebrows raised. 'Myrrh!'

Narmer had heard of myrrh. But no trader had brought any to Thinis in his lifetime.

The priests said that the gods loved myrrh above all the other scents that were burnt on their altars. They said myrrh could cure illness and drive away evil. No one even knew where myrrh came from, but the small brown balls were the most precious substance in the world.

Narmer suddenly imagined the effect that all these riches would have on the Yebu people who came with Berenib for the wedding feast. One look at all of this — one sniff of the cinnamon and myrrh — and they'd know just how rich and powerful this southern town was. A rich town means a well-defended town, he realised. That's why we show all our wealth at a feast: to keep our town safe.

The Trader spoke, smiling politely at the King. Nitho translated, 'My master says, "Which goods please Your Majesty?"'

The King hesitated, his eyes still fixed on the wealth before him. 'We would take them all, if we could. But I doubt there is enough grain in all our granaries to pay for them. I have no wish to leave our people hungry before the next harvest.'

Narmer could hear the smile in Nitho's voice as she translated the Trader's next words. 'Your concern does you credit, o wise and noble King. But my master feels it only right that such a great city as yours should have only the best, especially for the marriage of your most worthy son. Perhaps you could trade something that would leave the wheat and barley for the people?'

The King's hands caressed an ivory pot. 'What?'

'Gold,' Nitho translated.

Narmer started. How did Nitho know that they had a gold mine? More eavesdropping, he supposed.

The gold mine was out in the hills, beyond the River valley. Its location was a secret, known only to the King and his family, and a few trusted guards and servants who were well paid for their discretion.

Gold came from the sun god, Ra. Only the King and his family could wear gold amulets or bracelets, which reflected the sun's divine rays.

'For all of these treasures,' said Nitho calmly, 'my master asks for only enough gold to fill four cups.'

The King's face clouded. 'I am afraid we don't have ...' he began.

The Trader's gaze never left the King's face. He said something else, the words soft and full of promise.

'But my master says you have been kind to us poor strangers from the desert,' Nitho went on, her tones as silky as the Trader's. 'And as a gesture of friendship to our kind hosts, we will reduce the price. Three cups of gold and provisions to see us across the desert, and all these splendours are yours.'

The King's face cleared. Narmer knew as well as he did that the kingdom only had three cups of gold. It took many moons to dig the gold-bearing rock and carry it secretly to the River where the gold could be washed free.

'In that case ...' began the King.

Narmer leant forward. 'A quarter of a cup of gold.'

The others stared at him. His sudden interruption had surprised even himself. Yet it was as though he'd been watching a new game and suddenly understood its rules. And this was a game he could win — for Thinis.

For a moment Narmer thought the King was going to rebuke him, but his father said nothing.

The Trader kept his face impassive as Nitho translated. He glanced at Narmer and nodded to himself. He smiled faintly, then said something more.

'Surely you do not think wealth like this,' Nitho brushed her hands over the chest of myrrh, the panther skins, the cups, 'is worth a mere quarter cup of gold?'

Narmer's smile matched the Trader's. 'Of course not. Wealth like this is worth all the gold in the desert.'

He waited for Nitho to repeat his words then added, 'We are a poor town, even though we have given our best to our honoured guests. If we had three cups of gold we would give them to you. But we don't.'

Nitho's eyes widened above her scarf. She said something urgently to the Trader.

Aha, thought Narmer. You knew exactly how much gold we have, o Oracle who listens to the servants. I bet a cleft in the rocks isn't the only place where you're used to hiding to find out information.

'Our apologies,' said Nitho sweetly.

I've got you rattled, thought Narmer. She was starting to use her own voice now, thought he doubted anyone else had noticed.

'We understand your sad situation,' she went on. 'An eighth part of the goods, then, for a quarter of a cup of gold.'

Narmer shook his head. Neither his father nor his brother had any intention of interrupting him now, he realised. He wondered if Hawk even understood what an eighth part was. Hawk had no interest in numbers. They waited, intent on his words.

'A quarter cup for it all.' Narmer stood and lifted the box of myrrh, exaggerating its heaviness. 'Such a big box,' he said admiringly, as the Trader smiled, 'It would be heavy to carry all the way across the desert.'

'But . . .' began Nitho.

Narmer pressed on. 'That's where you're headed, isn't it? Back the way you came? Where there's no market for fine goods such as these?'

He put the chest down again regretfully. 'Father, we are not being fair to these kind people. We must not take up their time any longer. Let them take their wonderful goods and find a buyer who can pay what they are worth. Further along the River, perhaps . . .'

No one said anything. They all knew as well as Narmer that no other town along the River had gold to pay for goods like these. Min or Yebu might offer flint knives, barley or stone carvings. But none of those was worth carrying back across the Endless Desert.

The Trader grinned. He held up one finger and gestured at the goods.

'A half cup, then,' said Narmer. 'And food and water to see you through the desert to the coast.'

The Trader laughed. His whole face changed. I'm seeing it for the first time, thought Narmer. Up till now we've just seen the mask he wanted us to see.

The Trader nodded at Narmer, then said something to Nitho.

'My master agrees. He says,' said Nitho — and this time Narmer found it impossible to read the emotion behind the words — 'that it is a pity you are going to be a king. You would make an excellent trader. Your father is to be envied, for having such a son.'

The King burst out laughing too, partly at the joke and partly, Narmer supposed, in relief at getting the treasures for much less than he'd expected to pay for them.

'My son is more precious to me than any of these fine wares,' he said. He ruffled Narmer's hair. 'One day he will be the greatest king our town has ever seen. Won't you, my son?'

'Thank you, Father,' said Narmer, looking over at Nitho. But she was gazing at the lotus pool, as though waiting for a fish to break the surface.

One more night, he thought. Early tomorrow they'll be leaving, their donkeys packed, their water bags filled. Perhaps he could call at the guesthouse later today and say goodbye.

He glanced at her again. She was looking at the tiles on the colonnades now, as though admiring their pattern of egrets and fish.

What was the point? What would he say? And after tomorrow he would never see her again.

CHAPTER 8

Narmer got to sleep at last.

What did he care about one scarred girl? Especially one who had hidden from him and tricked him. He wouldn't think of Nitho. He'd think of Berenib, Berenib the beautiful. Just two new moons to go ...

His last thought, as he finally got to sleep, was that he hoped Berenib knew what to do on their wedding night ...

'Narmer! Wake up!'

Narmer sat straight up in alarm. 'What is it? Have the People of the Sand attacked?' But the Oracle had said they wouldn't attack till after harvest, he thought — and then he remembered: the Oracle was only Nitho ...

'Hippopotamus!'

Narmer blinked and woke up properly. Hawk was standing by the bed, his frog eyes wide in the moonlight.

Narmer swung his legs off the bed. 'Where?'

'Up by the top dyke. The flood must have stranded it there. It'll stamp the walls to mud by morning.'

'Have you called out the guards?'

'They're coming. They'll catch us up.'

There was something strange about Hawk's voice tonight. It's excitement, thought Narmer, pulling on his kilt. I've never heard Hawk sound excited before.

'You're coming too?' Narmer asked. Hawk rarely hunted, preferring life in the palace.

Hawk grinned. And that too was strange. 'If I'm with you then you won't be breaking your promise to Father. You won't be hunting alone. We'd better hurry,' he added, 'before it does any more damage.'

Narmer grabbed his spears as he went out the door.

The moon sailed across the night sky like a round loaf, sending a wash of silver across the River. The wind from the desert had cooled as it crossed the flood. The River smelt even more strongly now that the waters had receded, of rotting leaves, dung and unwary animals caught in the waters far upstream, as well as silt. Narmer slapped at a mosquito and then another.

The palace and the town were quiet. Not even the blue flicker of a castor oil lamp shone through the cracks of the mats that were hung over windows to keep out dust and insects. The only sounds were a few snores drifting down from sleepers who had made their beds up on the flat roofs, and the cry of a disturbed plover from the hills beyond the flood.

'This way,' whispered Hawk.

They began to run. Up the town's central street and onto the main dyke. Hawk was soon out of breath.

Narmer peered though the shadows. Hippos were hard to see at the best of times. Even in the moonlight it was almost impossible to spot a grey hide against a black sky, in even blacker water.

But they should have been able to hear the animal by now. Perhaps it was dozing, thought Narmer — just as Hawk called out behind him, 'Stop!'

'Is this the right place?' Narmer tried to make out shapes in the darkness. The water was rippled with moonlight, the dyke wall all mud and shadows.

'Down there!' Hawk pointed into the shallows, hanging back. Narmer had long suspected that Hawk was scared of animals, especially large ones.

Narmer waded into the water. But still nothing moved. Was the hippo sitting motionless against the bank? It was impossible to see. Was it —

The world exploded.

For precious seconds he wondered where he was, and what had happened. His mind had been focused on the hippopotamus. He hadn't thought of a crocodile.

Its first lunge trapped his leg. He screamed and twisted, so that he landed on his stomach in the mud, his head still out of the water, the great jaws still around his flesh.

'Help!' he shrieked. 'Hawk! Help!'

There was no answer.

The croc was shaking him now, back and forth. Then it slid into the mud, and the water rose around him as the monster dragged him down.

Down, down ... His fingers grasped frantically at the mud. He screamed again. This time the pain was too great for words.

Down under the water, the blackness choking him, the cold gripping him — all but his leg, which was a burst of fire. And then the creature rolled ...

Over, under, twisting him, turning. This was the death roll, from which nothing escaped.

His leg was agony. More than agony. His lungs were bursting, desperate for air. But he couldn't breathe. If he breathed he would drown, there in the murk and darkness. If he breathed the beast would have him. Not even his bones would be found.

And then it surfaced, dragging him along. Time for one quick gasp of air, then down again ...

Time slowed. It was as if his brain had all the time it needed now to calculate his last chance of escape.

This time he lashed out, twisted himself, trying to get his fingers into the beast's eyes. The crocodile seemed startled. Prey animals always went limp and passive in the water. They gave in to the will of the predator.

Not Narmer. Never Narmer. He thrust out again. Once again he had the feeling that the monster was shaken. This shouldn't be happening, hadn't ever happened; quarry never behaved this way. For just one instant the beast relaxed its grip. Narmer surged upwards. He had to get air! For one blessed moment he smelt mud and night-time, felt the air rush into his lungs.

Beside him the crocodile rose to the surface as well. It too needed to breathe. Narmer felt its leathery back against him; caught one glimpse of its teeth in the moonlight. And then he leapt, flinging himself towards the dyke wall, landing in the water again, but for the moment free, his feet pushing at the mud. No, one foot only, the other . . .

There was no time to think about the other . . .

Somehow, with one foot only, he struggled up onto the dyke, then fell onto his stomach in the mud. He couldn't get up, he couldn't run, but he could crawl . . .

He screamed again. Again there was no answer. Had Hawk run for help? Any moment now, thought Narmer, they'll come, with spears and javelins. They'll drive the beast away . . .

Something moved behind him, a slithering through the mud. The crocodile!

How far would it chase him? How fast could it go? A croc could grab its prey with lightning speed. But he'd never seen one run further than a few cubits.

He pushed his fingers deep into the mud — anything to help pull himself along faster. His breathing was too loud now to hear anything behind him — or was that his beating heart? His leg was on fire, but at the same time colder than the flood.

He had to run.

He stood up shakily. He hopped and staggered ahead, further, further, further. How could you run when one leg dragged behind you?

Narmer didn't know. He only knew that somehow he did it.

The night was cold. Hot. Empty, except for the beast behind him . . .

Along the dyke he limped. Further. Further. Further . . .

Then suddenly he knew that he had got away. The instinct of any hunted beast, perhaps, that knew it had made it to freedom. The croc had decided that there were easier meals to be had. There was an ox nearby, unwary, its muzzle in the water, drinking at the dyke . . .

And then Narmer fell.

This time he knew there was no rising. He reached down to touch his side. It was wet and warm — not from water, but blood.

He didn't dare to look. He just lay there gasping, falling into blackness . . .

Something moved above him. It was Hawk, his smile white in the moonlight. Narmer had never really seen his brother smile before.

And then the darkness won.

CHAPTER 9

They found him in the morning.

He had known little of the night. Brief glimpses, moonlight, mud and unbearable pain, then unconsciousness again.

Then suddenly voices, yells, a scream as someone saw his wounds, his name muttered in fearful tones from person to person. Then hands, gentle, but causing pain enough for darkness to close in once more, as they took him home to die.

Then nothing.

He awoke again in the palace. He was in his rooms, but the bed was different; underneath him was a pile of furs, covered with a linen cloth. Softer, smoother than his bed. Faces swam above him. Someone was crying. And then he heard his father's voice. There had never been anguish in his father's voice before.

'How did this happen? How?'

More darkness. He felt Seknut's hands upon him, just like in his childhood. It was she who was crying. But Seknut never cried. There was more pain as someone pressed his legs. No, not pain, what he felt was beyond pain. It was more like fire, as though his leg had been shoved into an oven.

'I can't stop the bleeding!' Was that Seknut's voice, or someone else's?

Narmer had never imagined cold could be like this. Cold that came from within him, not from the air, as his warmth and life flowed away.

He heard his father again, yelling orders to the priests, just like he shouted commands in war.

He could feel amulets pressed against his side. A voice muttered beside him, one of the priests, chanting a spell to Isis: 'Protect him from evil-wishers who are alive, from evil that is dead, or red . . .'

Somehow he knew the spell had no power, not over wounds like this. He had to speak. There was something he had to say. It had come to him at some point in that endless night, in the moments between thought and blackness. His lips moved, but no sound came.

'The Trader . . .' he tried to say.

Seknut's face bent low over his.

'The Trader.' How could he make her understand? Nothing in his life had been so hard. 'The Trader knows how . . .'

There was no strength to say more, to tell her, 'The Trader mended Nitho's leg. Perhaps he can mend mine.'

Would she understand?

Now a sandstorm, instead of darkness, swept him away. He saw red and white, then nothing . . .

* * *

Suddenly there was agony.

It was enough to wake him, bring him back from the nothing place, the cold place, the place of endless sleep.

Someone was holding his leg. For a moment he thought it was the crocodile again. And then he opened his eyes and looked into the Trader's face.

The Trader was holding something; it was an awl, Narmer realised, like the women used for sewing. There was thread as well. And suddenly the Trader pushed the awl into his leg so that it pierced through the skin.

Princes didn't scream. Princes were meant to bear everything in silence. But he screamed nonetheless.

The sandstorm thickened again. He heard the Trader's voice. Then Nitho's face bent over him, and she pinched his cheeks so hard they hurt.

How could you feel a pinch when your leg was in flames? But it was enough to keep him awake, to stop the sandstorm from sweeping him away.

'Stay with us,' ordered Nitho. It was the voice of the Oracle, the voice of his dreams. Narmer obeyed.

The pain seemed to last forever . . .

Finally he felt Nitho's hands spooning something into his mouth, something bitter, but tasting faintly of honey. Most of it dribbled down his chin. The spoon returned. This time Nitho held his head, to make it easier for him to swallow. The mixture trickled down his throat. He wanted to speak, but the room whirled.

And suddenly there was no pain.

It was dark when Narmer woke again, apart from a lamp flickering by his bed: a small flame on a tiny lake of oil. He heard snoring, and could see the dim bulk of the Trader sleeping on a pile of cushions in the corner. Bast was there too, sprawled over the Trader's feet as though the cushions belonged to her, not him.

Something moved beside him. Nitho. Her scarf was still across her face, but her dark eyes looked at him steadily.

She held a spoon to his lips again. 'Drink it,' she whispered. 'The poppy juice will make you sleep.'

'Nitho?' Again, the words were hardly there. But somehow she understood.

'Yes. It's me. Can you understand?'

He couldn't nod. He blinked instead. He forced his lips to move again. 'How bad?'

She looked at him, eyes wide in the lamplight, as though wondering how much to tell him. 'The top of your leg is gone, and half of your buttock. There are teeth marks on your lower leg. We've sewn up the worst of it, but the puncture wounds are deep. There'll be fever, but we'll do what we can.'

'Die?' whispered Narmer. She would tell him the truth, he knew. Oracles never lied . . .

'I don't know.' There was honesty in her voice. 'We'll do our best.' She hesitated. 'There's a wound on your face too, a deep one. But not from teeth. From a stick maybe, in the mud.' And then, 'You've lost a lot of blood. You need to drink. The poppy will take away your pain.'

No, thought Narmer, not take it away. The pain was part

of him now. But at least the poppy made it feel like the pain belonged to someone else.

And then he slept.

Time passed in a blur. Seknut muttered prayers to Bes, her favourite household god, beside his bed. Nitho, her hands cool on his hot skin, spooned liquid into his mouth, or simply sat holding his hand, as the pain washed back and forth.

The smell of blood was constant. Then there was a new smell of rotting flesh. Narmer glimpsed dead skin in a bowl by the bed and knew it was his, as the Trader's hands worked on him again and again smearing his wounds with a mixture of honey and myrrh and aloe. There had been garlic and crocodile dung in the mixture at first, which stank and had stung. The Trader made him drink teas, too: horrible messes of ox liver and raw eggs and onions, pounded smooth, with mint and sycamore seeds and more garlic.

His father's face hovered above him. Or was that a dream? Seknut whispered a spell: 'O Son of Pain, who brings the fever and the anguish . . .'

Once he woke to see Bast peering over him, her eyes pale gold in the moonlight. But it was Nitho's hand that held her. It was almost as though the two of them were guarding him. Somehow, thought Narmer vaguely, they were keeping death away.

Days passed. No, not days. Days were defined by meals, at such and such a time, and sleep at night. This was just . . . time. Time and poppy and pain.

And then less poppy and more pain. And somehow, the realisation that he was going to live.

CHAPTER 10

There had been no more poppy this morning. So when the King arrived Narmer was fully awake, for the first time since the pain had begun to rule his life.

His father had been alone when he came before, usually at night, to sit with his son in the darkness. But today he came as the King, attended by his guards, his sandal bearer and his fanners, with their giant ostrich-feather fans. He waved them away at the door and entered alone.

Narmer watched as Nitho and the Trader bowed, picked up their medicine bowls, and left. The cat stalked out after them, her tail waving.

'I'm sorry, Father,' Narmer whispered.

The King touched his cheek gently. 'I'm sorry too, my son. More sorry than you can ever know. This was why I made you promise never to hunt alone. You promised —'

'But I wasn't alone!' Narmer rasped. 'Hawk was with me!'

'Hawk was asleep in the palace. The first he knew of the accident was when they brought you back.'

'He told me there was a hippo by the top dyke! We went together! He must have run away and left me!'

'Hawk knew nothing of this.' His father's voice was firm beneath its gentleness. 'You must have dreamt it in your delirium.' Or lied. The words hung in the air, almost as loud as if he'd said them.

He wanted to yell out, *Hawk did this to me! Hawk tried to kill me!* But he was too weak to say the words. Words like those would mean a battle. He would fight that war when he was stronger. Hawk will not get away with this, he told himself.

His father took his hand. 'My son ...' The King hesitated, as though he too were looking for the strength to find the words that must be said. 'You are going to live,' he said at last. 'But you may never walk again. Or run. Or hunt. Or fight.

'Narmer, do you remember before ... before the crocodile? I told you that a king lives for his people, not himself. So today I have to ask you to be a king, while you're still a prince ... to sacrifice yourself for your people, just as you might do in battle.'

Narmer stared at him, not understanding. Then comprehension dawned. 'No!' he whispered desperately.

'My son ... My dear son ... The people of Thinis need a king who can lead them in war. A king the other towns will fear.'

The King's voice grew stronger. 'I will not — cannot — make Hawk my heir instead of you. The people respect you. Love you. They would never give Hawk their love and obedience if they thought I had taken the kingship away from you. When I died they would be waiting, always waiting, wondering if you would try to take the throne from your brother.'

The King paused. And then he added, 'So it has to be your choice. A true king's decision: to give that kingship up.'

The cold flooded Narmer's body. It was as though his blood were seeping out of him again. But this time, he thought, it is my life, not my blood.

To give up everything he was. No longer Guardian Prince of Thinis. No longer heir to his father's throne.

And to give it up to Hawk! Hawk, who had schemed to kill him, to gain the kingship for himself!

It was almost unthinkable. But there was no one else. The King's words hung in the silent air.

Narmer glanced out the door. All he could see was part of the courtyard: the lily pool, the tiles. But it would be his last glimpse of his future kingdom. Did he really have a choice?

He took a deep breath. His voice must remain steady. He struggled to sit up. It took his whole strength. But he would not say this lying like a child in bed.

His father helped him. But the King's hands shook as they arranged the pillows to support his son, and tears ran down his cheeks.

'I resign all claims to the kingship.'

Seknut brought him stuffed dates and honeyed lotus seeds, treats that he'd loved when he was small. He nibbled a few to make her happy, to let her feel that there was something — anything — that she could do for him.

But there was nothing. Everything he was had gone.

64

His father sent him a robe of panther skin and ordered quails to be trapped and roasted to tempt his son to eat.

Narmer fed them to the cat. How could he eat at a time like this?

Bast was his main companion these days. Humans wanted to comfort him, but the cat just wanted to eat his dinner.

It still seemed strange to give an animal a name, Bast — as though she were a person, not a wildcat. Of course geese could be tamed and sheep followed their shepherds. But to have an animal indoors? Unheard of. But he had to admit that once you got to know her Bast started to seem like a person too. Self-possessed, always ready for another meal. He also remembered how Bast had been ready to attack him when he might have threatened Nitho.

Would Bast do that for me? he wondered. Sometimes — just sometimes — he dreamt of watching her rip open his brother as she had the lizards, all that time ago.

How could he have been so stupid? Was he so used to love and admiration that he never noticed his brother's hate and envy?

Night after night he tossed and sweated, longing to tear that smile from his brother's face, just as Hawk had torn his future from him.

It was hardest of all today. Because today Hawk, Prince of Thinis, was marrying Berenib, Princess of Yebu. The King of Yebu had sent his daughter to marry the heir of Thinis, and it seemed he didn't care who the heir was. Hawk or Narmer, it was all the same to him.

Hawk the heir. Hawk the victorious. Or Narmer the cripple. Narmer the nothing.

Outside people cheered. The air was filled with the sound of flutes and drums, and the smoke of roasting meat and baking bread.

But in his room Narmer watched the cat wash herself with one great paw, and almost wished he had died.

Hawk came to see him two days later, while the Trader was changing Narmer's bandages. It was the first time his brother had visited him alone. Before he had always been with the King, and attended by guards and servants.

Hawk still looked amused, but also taller somehow, and his face more vivid, as though there had been a cloak over him before. Now the real man shone through.

Today the prince was decked out in more gold than even his father had ever worn. Even his long kilt was trimmed with gold. His eyes were rimmed with kohl. Gold gleamed on his wrists and arms, and there was a familiar gold amulet on his chest.

That's mine! Narmer wanted to cry. But it belonged to the heir of Thinis, not to him. All he could do was lie on his bed, propped up by cushions, while his brother towered over him.

'Greetings, little brother,' said Hawk calmly, waving the Trader out of the room. The Trader cast a sharp look at Narmer, then obeyed.

'Congratulations,' said Narmer. He was relieved to find his voice was steady. He tried to keep his face as expressionless as Hawk's had once been.

'Thank you.'

Hawk pulled up a chair and sat down. He caressed its arms with his long soft fingers and smiled at Narmer. 'I must have this taken to my rooms,' he said. 'You won't need a chair now. I'll have a cushion sent in its place.'

A chair for the heir, and cushions for everyone else. Narmer watched his brother for a moment, then he said, 'You knew the crocodile was there.'

Hawk smiled at him enigmatically. 'What are you talking about?'

Narmer ignored him. 'I was too weak to explain it to Father before. And now of course I can never tell him.'

'Why is that?' Hawk's voice was light. But his eyes were watchful.

'Thinis needs to trust its king. So I will be loyal. For Thinis's sake, not yours.'

'I'm glad,' said Hawk pleasantly. He might have been talking about cucumbers for breakfast. 'You'll make me an excellent vizier. You needn't worry that there won't be enough for you to do. All that interest in dykes and building walls can be put to good use. And I ... I shall be king. As I always should have been.'

Narmer wanted to rage at him. Scream at him. Vow revenge.

But he was powerless. And Hawk knew it.

For Thinis, he repeated to himself. For Thinis.

'My regards to your wife,' he said at last, trying to keep the bitterness from his voice. 'I wish her well in her marriage.'

'Thank you.' Hawk smiled at him again. 'She is as beautiful as they say, you know. She wanted to visit you, but I said no. Your scars are quite horrible, you know. We don't want to give her nightmares.' He lifted his hand in farewell.

'Recover soon, little brother. I am sure I'll find a way to make you useful.'

He smiled again, and strolled from the room.

'I could poison him if you like.'

It was Nitho. She must have been hiding behind the door curtain, Narmer realised. 'I could slip a little something into his beer. He wouldn't die for days. No one would ever know.'

Nitho was carrying another noxious mixture, in a big pottery mug trimmed with black, with hunting scenes on the outside. Her scarf had come free, showing her whole face, with its bright twisted scar. The cat stalked after her, as though hoping that the mug held food.

Was Nitho serious? Narmer wondered. But it didn't really matter. He shook his head. 'No.'

'Why not? He's a poisonous reptile. Worse than a reptile. Snakes only attack for food, or if they're scared.'

'But he's the only other son my father has.'

'Then without him you'd be the heir again.'

'No. Without him there'd be chaos. Every soldier who thought he should lead the army would wonder if he could be king. I can't even walk, much less lead the army. What use is a king who has to be carried in a litter?'

'You'll walk,' said Nitho, 'even if I have to pull you with a rope to make you take your first steps.'

'*Mrrrww*,' agreed Bast. She sat on the chair that Hawk had just vacated and began to wash herself.

'You won't be here. You and your master have stayed so long already.'

'Your father has paid us well for it: the rest of the gold that you bargained us out of.' She smiled briefly, twisting her scar even further. 'Perhaps that is the great fortune my master's oracle spoke of. We'll stay to see you on your feet, of course. The rest is up to you.'

She looked at him steadily for a moment. 'You can do it, o great Prince Narmer. If I can learn to walk on half a leg then you can too. As for your face . . .' She shrugged. 'It's not as bad as mine. At least your scar will fade.'

She handed him the mug. Narmer sipped. He wished she'd wipe his face, as she used to do, or even hold his hand. But she never touched him these days, except to help the Trader change his dressings.

Seknut bustled in with food for him. Nitho left, and the cat followed her; Bast knew there was no chance of getting food from Seknut.

Seknut sat with him while he ate, then she left him too.

It was a luxury to be alone, after so many days of always having someone in his room, listening to his breathing or his mutterings. Narmer lay there, looking at the ceiling and thinking.

No more golden future. No more kingship.

So what was left?

One leg that worked. Another that might work, at least a bit, given time.

A scar on his face Nitho told him would fade.

A talent for hunting he couldn't use, a gift for administration he didn't want to use. There was no way he could be his brother's vizier. Not even for Thinis.

Suddenly he realised he was free. If he was no longer the heir then he was no longer bound by duty. It was as though the ropes that had bound him to Thinis had snapped. He felt light as a leaf that could fly in the wind.

But where to? What did he *want* to do? What *could* he do?

He knew his numbers. He could write the tallies almost as well as a priest. The priesthood, then? At least the gods weren't subject to his brother, nor were those who served them.

But which god could he serve? Osiris, god of the Underworld? No, he'd felt Osiris's breath on his cheek. He wanted no more of Osiris.

Hathor, the cow goddess? But she was the King's special guardian. That thought hurt too much also.

Horus, falcon god of the sky?

Seth, the god of storm and war and violence?

How could he serve at a shrine to those who had let this happen to him? He couldn't even sing or strum a lyre ...

He wouldn't cry. He *couldn't* cry. He was too empty for tears.

Nothing left. His position, his future, even the health and the handsomeness he had taken for granted ...

A breeze blew through the door. It brought the scent of the desert, along with a scatter of sand. The servants would need to sweep tomorrow, he thought idly ...

And suddenly he knew what he could do.

CHAPTER 11

The Season of Emergence (Late Winter)

Narmer waited another half moon, till he had managed to stand up by himself for a few brief heartbeats, and was strong enough to sit upright on his pillows the whole day instead of lying like a baby. He waited till the Trader came with Nitho one morning, to change his bandages.

He waited till he had borne it all without a sound — the dead flesh and scabs pulled off with the linen cloths, the honey mixture smeared on the wounds, which still seeped blood and ooze at the edges.

And then he asked them.

Nitho sat back on her heels, the soiled linen still in her hands. 'You want *what*?'

'To join you. To serve your master. To learn to be a trader too.' Narmer almost smiled for the first time since he had met the crocodile.

Nitho sounded too shocked to even translate. Behind her the Trader waited, peering at Narmer through his dried-grape eyes, as inscrutable as ever.

'You heard me,' he said to Nitho. 'Could you ask the Trader for me?' His heart was leaping as though he were about to jump off a cliff. But he kept his voice steady.

'But you can't!' Nitho fought to gain control of herself under her scarf. 'Prince Narmer, you don't understand,' she added more formally. 'You'll be leaving your home forever! We'll never come this way again!'

'I understand that,' said Narmer slowly.

'Do you?' She gestured at Narmer's room, the hangings on the wall. 'You've only seen us living like you do, as guests of the palace. But my master isn't rich, even if you think he carries riches. We don't live like this most of the time.'

'I know ...' began Narmer.

'How can you, here in your safe River valley? Have you any idea what the desert is really like? What it's like to face people who have never met a trader before, who believe a stranger must be an enemy and enemies must be killed, and to have only seconds to convince them to let you live? Do you know how to face people of strange towns and stranger languages and persuade them to take your wares? Knowing that if you fail they may steal everything you have? Or, almost as bad, send you on your way with no food or water, and no guides to find any?'

'Of course I don't know,' said Narmer quietly. 'But I want to.'

Nitho's big eyes gazed intently at him over her scarf. Then she turned to the Trader and began to speak.

Narmer tried to follow their conversation. He had picked up a little of the Trader's language now. What was Nitho saying so vehemently? Was she arguing that he should come? Or stay?

As usual the Trader's expression was impossible to read. But somehow Narmer didn't think he looked surprised.

Finally Nitho turned to him again. 'My master says, "Why should we take a boy who stumbles instead of walks? What can you offer us in return?"'

Narmer had thought of this over the days and nights he had lain here.

Even the bracelets on his arms were Hawk's now. Nor did he have other languages, like Nitho. But there was one thing he did have.

'I beat your master out of two and a half cups of gold,' he said. 'Next time I will be on his side and get the gold for him.'

Nitho translated. The Trader grinned and spoke to her briefly.

'He agrees,' said Nitho.

'What? Just like that?' Narmer had been prepared to argue, even plead, to bargain for this just like he had bargained with the Trader before.

'My master says,' Nitho continued, 'that if you're not worth your bread we can just leave you in the desert for the jackals. No loss to us either way.' But she looked startled too, as though the Trader's words had surprised her.

Narmer stared at the Trader. Was he serious? The man's eyes crinkled, as though he were laughing at a joke no one else had heard.

Was this some kind of test?

'Good,' Narmer said evenly. 'Then it's a fair trade. No loss on either side.'

'Except your life, perhaps,' said Nitho drily.

Narmer shrugged. At the moment his life didn't seem much to risk.

Seknut cried. Her face screwed up like a pomegranate left too long in the sun. She covered her face with her hands to try to hide her sobs.

'Into the Endless Desert! No one survives the desert!'

'The People of the Sand do.'

Narmer felt like crying too. But he hadn't cried before — when the crocodile attacked; when the King made Hawk his heir. He wouldn't let himself cry now, either. If only he could take Seknut with him! But an old woman would never survive the desert. And a Trader's apprentice did not have servants.

Seknut shook her head without replying, the tears streaming down her cheeks. The People of the Sand were barbarians. The River was the only world she knew.

But there is another world beyond the River, thought Narmer. A world of giant boats and lands of strange treasures. A new excitement was growing within him.

He told his father privately, kneeling on his cushion before the throne.

He expected the King to object, to plead with him not to go. But he didn't. Instead his father sat silently on his throne, while the noises of the palace lapped over them: the songs of the women in the kitchen courtyard, the sounds of their chopping, the cry of a plover near the River.

Finally the King said, 'Good.'

The word hurt, even more than the teeth of the crocodile. But Narmer understood. Even crippled, he was a threat to Hawk. The new rule would be easier with Narmer gone. The King had spoken, not his father.

'I wish ...' Suddenly it was his father talking, not the King. 'I wish it could be different. If I could give my life for yours, my legs to the crocodile in exchange for yours ...' His father's fingers gripped the chair arms so tightly the knuckles were white.

Was he going to say 'I would give anything for you to be my heir, not Hawk'?

Suddenly Narmer knew he couldn't bear to hear the words. Nor should a king say them.

Instead Narmer used his crutch to lift himself from his cushion and threw his arms round his father. It was unheard of; even as the heir he had never touched the King unbidden.

He felt his father tremble as he returned the hug.

Yes, it was better that he left.

The King gave the Trader more gold — all the gold his servants could mine in the moon before they left. It seemed strange to Narmer that the gold went to the Trader, not to him. But he was no longer Prince of Thinis, and the Trader was his master now. It was something that would take a while to get used to.

The King gave them provisions too: dried meat and fruit, parched grain, travel bread baked in the oven till it was hard. He would have given them more, but the porters could only carry so much.

Seknut fussed over Narmer to distract herself from her grief, weaving him a new kilt and ordering him new sandals, as though the best clothes she could find would protect him from the demons of the outside world.

The night before they left, the King held a feast as splendid as the one for Hawk and Berenib's wedding.

It was hard to feel the people's eyes on him, gazing at his scars, his crippled leg. It was hard to hear their farewells.

'You will always be our Golden One,' cried Rintup the rope maker. There were tears in the man's eyes.

No, thought Narmer. You are mourning the loss of the boy I used to be, not the one I am now. The Golden One has vanished.

And in his place . . . who knows?

It was hard to watch Berenib, who was as beautiful as he'd expected, trying not to look at his scarred face. It was even harder for Narmer to see his brother, with gold ornaments on his neck and arms and forehead, sitting on the stool that had been his, at the King's side. But it only strengthened his resolve to go.

That night in bed he was dozing, too keyed up to sleep properly, when a shadow crept into his room.

For a moment he thought it might be Hawk, come to finish him off. He froze, pretending to sleep. But then he realised it was his father.

The King sat on the chair by Narmer's bed. He didn't attempt to wake his son, but simply sat there in the darkness. And Narmer found he too was content simply to lie there, breathing evenly, watching his father in return from under his lashes.

What could they have talked about if he had shown he was awake? What words would bridge their loss — the loss of a kingdom, the loss of a father, the loss of a son? Both knew they would probably never see each other again.

So both stayed silent in the darkness. Narmer dozed. Perhaps the King did too. And before the dawn the King slipped away.

CHAPTER 12

The Trader's party left in the predawn light, with only the King and Seknut to farewell them. They were under way before anyone in the town but the bakers was stirring, lighting the fires for the day's bread, or the occasional woman with a fretful, wakeful child, looking out her windows as they passed.

Bast was nowhere to be seen. But Nitho had assured him that the cat would be waiting for them beyond the town. Cats were good, she said, at 'following in front'.

They were heading for a city called Punt, according to Nitho, to spend the gold from Thinis on more myrrh. Then they'd take the myrrh to Ka'naan to trade it for copper, then take the copper to Sumer to trade for yet more gold.

This, it seemed, was how traders made their living.

The porters carried the spears and tents, the water bags, and the deerskin bags of parched grain and dates, dried meat, figs and raisins, travel bread and lotus seeds, chattering away in their own strange tongue. Neither the Trader nor Nitho carried more than a small pack, and an even smaller water bag.

Two of the porters also carried Narmer's litter, a chair fastened to two tent poles. He was glad there were so few people around to see him carried like a baby through the streets where he had once run while the people smiled and bowed. The jiggling movement of the litter hurt his leg and made him feel a bit sick, like being in a fishing boat on the River. But he welcomed the pain. Anything to stop the deeper pain of thinking about what he was leaving behind.

They passed through the streets of the town, with their familiar smells of human dung and baking bread, then out onto the road through the fields. The flood had subsided, leaving rich black mud that was already turning to dust. The first shoots of wheat and barley had poked through the soil now. Soon the gardeners would carry buckets of water on yokes over their shoulders for the vegetables and the fruit trees. Fishermen would take their boats out onto the River; women would wash their clothes in its shallows; and children would drive flocks of geese or goats out to graze, or wave fans in the orchards to scare away the birds.

But he would see none of it.

I will not cry! he told himself desperately. He held himself upright on his chair, his face frozen to stop the tears that tried to fall. I won't look back, I won't!

But he did. He saw the River flashing silver, the early smoke rising from the town. Thinis had never looked so beautiful.

This land had been his life. All he had ever hoped for or imagined was here.

Now he would never see Thinis again.

Houses gave way to plots of grain and orchards. And then the rich moist floodlands were behind them. They climbed into the hills, dry and hot as the baker's oven.

They stopped at midday at a water seep: a thin film of surprisingly cool water that dripped from a rock into a pool no bigger than a cupped hand.

Bast headed to the water and began to drink, then pounced on a lizard that had been unwise enough to try to drink there too. The porters put Narmer's chair down in the shade of a rock, then went to replenish their water bags.

Narmer leant against the cool stone and closed his eyes. He felt exhausted already. Even though he had been sitting up this past moon, even trying a few cautious steps, it was far more tiring to brace his body against the jiggling of the litter for hours at a time.

This would be his life now, he thought dismally. Hobbling to his litter, leaning on someone's shoulder. Crippled forever ...

'Hungry?' Nitho squatted beside him, holding out a handful of dates. She had left off her scarf as soon as they were beyond Thinis, but she still wore the headdress. The Trader had insisted that Narmer wear one too. He was grateful now. The cloth at least kept off the worst of the sun.

Narmer shook his head. 'No, thank you.'

Nitho no longer called him Prince, he realised. He supposed no one ever would again.

'You'd better drink something, at least.' This time she held out a damp water bag.

Narmer drank from it. The water tasted of goatskin. He'd have liked to spill some of the cool water over his head, but water was precious now. Was this still River water? he wondered. Or had Nitho filled it from the pool? The River had given him everything he was — his food, his kingdom, his life's blood. Now he would never drink its waters again.

The Trader got up and barked out an order. The porters gathered their spears and began to pick up the baggage. Narmer struggled to his feet and started hobbling towards his chair.

'No,' the Trader said to him.

Narmer stared. Had he misunderstood? Nitho had been teaching him the Trader's language, but he still had a lot to learn.

The Trader's face showed no expression. 'You will walk,' he said firmly. 'Not ride.'

'But — but I can't!' He turned to Nitho, pleading, 'Nitho, tell him! Explain to him!'

Nitho's face was impassive too. 'He is your master now,' she said quietly. 'If he says walk, you walk.'

'But there's no way I can keep up with you!'

Had the Trader really been serious when he'd said they'd leave him in the desert? Narmer tried to calculate. Thinis was still only a morning's walk away. Surely he could make it back again! Limping, dusty, bedraggled, crawling perhaps . . .

He would rather die, and have the crows pick out his eyes.

'Walk,' said the Trader again. He held out a walking stick. The dark eyes were kind, but the wrinkled face inscrutable.

Narmer took the stick and began to hobble forward.

It was agony. His good leg took half his weight, the stick the other half. His bad leg refused to move by itself. He had to swing his body every time he took a step, so it would force his leg to swing too.

Step, swing, step, swing, step — it was as though fire played along his muscles. Step, step, step . . .

The sand burnt his feet. They had lost their toughness during the months in bed. But sandals were too cumbersome for walking far.

The others were getting further and further ahead. Narmer forced himself to go faster, his bare feet pushing frantically through the sand.

Step, swing, step, swing, step . . .

And slowly he realised that the agony had eased, just a little. That each time he swung his leg it moved a little more easily. That yes, he was finally walking . . .

Step, swing, step, swing, step, swing . . .

Sweat poured down his face. He didn't dare look at the others now to see how far ahead they were. It didn't matter, he thought grimly. If necessary he'd walk all night to catch up to them. Anything rather than return home a failure. Step, swing, step, swing . . .

'Narmer! Narmer!'

For a moment he hardly heard the words. Then the mist cleared before his eyes and he saw Nitho in front of him. She was holding out a water bag. The porters stood beside her with his chair.

'You did well,' she said gently. 'But that's enough. Drink now, then ride. You can walk again tomorrow.'

'I walked! I really walked!'

'Of course you did.' Her crooked smile was as wide as the River. 'The crocodile couldn't stop you, and neither will your leg. You can do anything you put your mind to, Narmer. Anything at all.'

And for a moment, there on the chair, with his leg shaking uncontrollably and triumph in his heart, he believed her. And it felt better than all the cheers and flattery in Thinis.

CHAPTER 13

A night, trying to sleep in a goatskin cloak, feeling the teeth of the rocks beneath. The stars wheeling above him in the clear desert sky, seeming so close he felt he could poke them with a stick. Oats for breakfast and half a day of jolting in the chair ...

They were out of the hills and into the real desert now.

Narmer had never been more than half a day from the green safety of the River, with its water and its wildlife. Out here there was neither.

The first thing he'd noticed was the light. It was pure white, out here away from the green River valley. The sun was so strong it seemed to bleach all the colour from the world. White light all around him, white light reflecting off quartz in the rocks, off sand.

The next thing he noticed was the space. The desert filled the world from horizon to horizon, with no human thing to break the monotony.

And then he noticed the noise.

He'd thought the desert would be silent. It wasn't. The sand rustled; in other stretches rocks creaked underfoot.

The wind was always howling somewhere past the horizon, even when the air around them was still.

But even in the Endless Desert, it seemed, there was grass, thin tufts sheltered by clumps of rocks, and the occasional seep of water, trickling into the sand or forming tiny puddles in the rock.

By now Narmer was getting to know the porters too, the big men who carried the baggage, put up the tents and, hopefully, frightened off any passers-by who might be tempted to steal their goods — or their lives.

Narmer had assumed that the Trader had hired his men on the journey. But it seemed that they were from Sumer too: Akkadians, the dark-skinned early inhabitants of the land between the rivers.

Narmer had heard of Sumer, but it had never quite seemed real before, just another story from places far away. Now, listening to the porters' strange language, Sumer became part of the new world he had to learn about.

Portho the porter with the scar on his shoulder, was the oldest. He had worked as a boy for the Trader's father, who, it seemed, had been a trader too. Portho could tie a piece of cord around his upper arm and flex his muscles so it snapped, and could whirl a stick in tinder to light a fire faster than anyone Narmer had ever seen.

Nid was the tallest, a giant of a man. He had lost his eye in a scuffle with tribesmen to the east. He munched grass stems as he walked, and one of his teeth was worn down further than the rest from his chewing.

Jod was the youngest, and smaller than the other two — though still half as tall again as any man in Thinis. But he had a soft voice of authority that the other guards obeyed even when the wind blew sand into their faces, and humans and animals alike were cranky.

The porters mostly chattered among themselves, in their own language, and the Trader seemed to enjoy silence. But most days Nitho talked to Narmer as she walked beside his chair. She was still teaching him Sumerian, but they spoke of other things as well.

It was Nitho who helped him climb a dune to watch a desert hare whirling in the sand, circling and prancing as though it had decided to dance with the wind. It was Nitho who told him stories of their trading expeditions to Ka'naan for copper or for tin in far-off Khorassan, where Nitho had seen a strange woman with hair the colour of the sand and eyes like bits of sky.

As Prince of Thinis Narmer had never had a friend. Was this what it might have been like, he wondered, to have a brother or sister who was a companion, instead of one who plotted to steal your throne? The friendship and adventure made him forget the loss of Thinis for a time — almost, at any rate.

And every day, whenever he looked up, Narmer would find the Trader's eyes upon him, bright in their setting of dark wrinkles, inscrutable.

What was the Trader thinking? Narmer could understand some of his speech now. But the Trader spoke little, leaving the routine of setting up camp to the porters.

'Is he always like this?' Narmer asked Nitho one afternoon as she walked beside his chair.

'What do you mean?'

'So quiet. He always seems to be ...' Narmer was going to say 'looking at me', but he substituted 'thinking'. 'He's not sorry he let me come, is he?'

'He's quieter than usual,' admitted Nitho, 'but of course he doesn't regret bringing you.'

Still, Narmer wondered.

Who was this man he had entrusted his future to? A trader's life had seemed so simple back in the safety of Thinis. Now, in the emptiness of the desert, Narmer realised how little he knew.

At least he had grown used to the caravan's routine. Each day they set off in the dim pre-dawn light, before it grew too hot. They travelled till midday, when they rested in shade if there was any to be found, or draped the tents across the poles if there wasn't, to keep off the sun and protect them from the worst of the afternoon's heat. In the late afternoon they walked again till the sun began to set. They ate at dawn and dusk: handfuls of dates or dried jujubes, or bread that Nitho made by dripping a little water into the bag of flour, flattening out the dough and baking it on the rocks or sand at mid-afternoon when they were hottest.

Narmer was amazed the first time he tasted one of these small flat cakes. It was cooked right through and the sand brushed straight off the crust. They tasted of the desert, of Nitho's hands and, just occasionally, of cat.

Bast was always there, but never quite with them. She roamed just out of sight, except at dawn and dusk, when she sat by Nitho gnawing at her food. She seemed to expect to be fed whatever the humans ate. But sometimes in the morning there was a small gift outside Nitho's tent: the half-chewed head of a desert lizard or a splodge of mouse guts, and once what Nitho swore was the tail of a cobra.

Narmer walked twice a day now. He could even put his full weight momentarily on his damaged leg.

And every day, Thinis and his life as a prince fell further behind.

They had been travelling for almost a moon when the strangers appeared on the horizon: black dots in the haze of the midday heat, so that at first Narmer wasn't sure they were really there. But slowly they grew larger, and larger still.

'People of the Sand,' said Nitho warily, shading her eyes from the glare.

Narmer snorted. 'People of the Sand are worthless. They just wander about, hunting — or stealing from other people. They tried to attack Thinis two floods ago. They don't build anything, or grow anything.'

The Trader looked at him with one of his small smiles. 'Is that so?'

Portho muttered something, staring anxiously at the strangers, his accent still too strong for Narmer to understand.

'War party,' agreed the Trader.

'How can you tell?'

'There are too many for a hunting party, and they're all men. If they were just moving from oasis to oasis there'd be women and children too.'

'Are they going to attack us?'

The Trader shrugged. 'That's up to you.'

'What do you mean?' demanded Narmer. 'Sir,' he added as an afterthought. It was hard to remember that he now had a master.

The Trader's lips stretched into a smile. 'They're heading towards us. That means they're either planning to fight us, or are curious and want to know who we are. Probably they haven't decided which.'

Narmer looked at the approaching men.

'You wanted to be a trader,' said his master calmly. 'This is where you start. Make them believe that it's better to trade with us than fight us.'

'How? They're People of the Sand! Thieves! All they have to do is kill us and they can take everything we have anyway!'

'Exactly,' said the Trader.

'Master!' said Nitho urgently. 'He's not ready!'

The Trader lifted his water skin and took a drink before answering her. 'I think he is.'

Narmer stared at him. How could the Trader risk the lives of everyone just to see whether Narmer could manage by himself?

The Trader raised an eyebrow, as though he knew what Narmer was thinking. 'Every time we trade,' he said, 'we're at the mercy of strangers. Your father could have taken us prisoner and stolen our goods, instead of paying us with gold. Every trade is a challenge and a danger.'

'So this is a lesson?' asked Narmer slowly.

'Of course.' The Trader gave another of his small smiles. His teeth seemed long and white for his age. 'All of life is a lesson,' he added. 'But for a moment, remember that a trade takes two sides. Both have to have something to give.'

Narmer bit his lip, his panic growing. What did People of the Sand have to trade? They carried nothing but their weapons. And what could the Trader give the People of the Sand? The strangers would have no use for gold, and the Trader's people needed everything else in their luggage to survive here in the desert.

Narmer looked around their caravan, at the porters whispering worriedly among themselves, at Bast stalking along two sandhills away. Nitho looked at him uncertainly, then nodded, as though she had decided to trust him, and fastened her scarf over her face again.

Were they really leaving it all to him? So this was the life of a trader: bargaining not just for gold but for life or death.

But he wasn't a trader yet! What could he show these men that would make their eyes gleam, like his father's had at the brown curls of myrrh? He was just a boy with scars and hopes ...

And suddenly he knew.

A linen cloth was spread across the sand and a small pot set down in the middle as the strangers approached.

There were perhaps forty of them, bare legged, with faces carved by sun and wind, and stiff, badly cured camel hide twisted about their hips. A few carried spears or slingshots. The rest carried rough wooden clubs.

Narmer gazed at them, fascinated despite the danger. He had never seen any of the People of the Sand up close before. He had been too young to fight the last time they attacked Thinis, and his father had decided that People of the Sand made poor servants. Any who were captured were slaughtered or sold to other towns like Min, where the King relied on slaves for much of the work.

Memories of home stabbed through him once again. Was the rest of his life to be spent bargaining with barbarians like these?

He could smell them already. These people stank.

They muttered among themselves as they gazed at the travellers sitting on the sand, looking as if they met bands of desert warriors every day. Jod, Nid and Portho had even left their spears on the ground — though still within reach.

Narmer stood up as the men approached, using his stick to keep himself steady. He bowed slowly, giving them time to take in the sight of Bast, purring as Nitho scratched her ears, the relaxed men lounging around the pot.

'We greet you, o brave men of the endless sands,' he said politely, and waited for Nitho to translate.

The men stared, first at him and then at Nitho as she spoke to them. But their eyes stayed blank, as though they didn't understand anything she said. Nitho said something else, then listened to the mutterings of the men.

'Sorry,' she whispered. 'I don't know their language.'

'But you know every language!' hissed Narmer.

'No, I don't. No one does!' she whispered back, exasperated. 'How many languages do you think there are in the world? Five? Ten? There must be thousands!'

Narmer felt a shiver of fear inside him. But he forced

himself to keep smiling, then pointed to the small pot in the middle of the smooth white linen cloth.

It was carved from smooth alabaster, and whiter than the sand around them. Inside was a dirty green liniment.

The strangers peered at it, unimpressed. Their muttering increased. One raised his spear and said something urgently to the others.

The meaning was clear: *Let's kill them now, before they have time to pick up their spears.*

Narmer held up his hand. Then slowly, very slowly, he lifted up his kilt. His scars glared red and purple in the desert light.

The strangers gasped. How could anyone have survived a wound like this?

Narmer lowered his kilt and pointed at the liniment, then at the Trader.

The mutters were different now. What would warriors need more than anything else? An ointment that could cure their wounds. And these people — these powerful people with their tame wildcat — had the secret.

The warrior leader gestured to the pot. Narmer smiled again, a smile as calm, he hoped, as the Trader's. As though he bargained with armed strangers every day, and thought nothing of it. He held up a water bag, then pointed at the pot again.

Take us to water, and you can have this.

The strangers chattered again. Then they began to smile.

It wasn't much of an oasis. A stand of date palms, their tops shaggy and dusty from the wind. The feathery leaves of tamarisk trees, shading a wrinkle of water forced to the surface by the band of rock that reared up through the sand, forming a slight cliff to one side. But it was enough for them all to drink deeply.

There was dried camel dung around the waterhole, which meant they had fuel for a fire. Portho twirled two sticks together to get a spark onto this tinder, then Nitho tended the flames, setting a pot of the barley they'd brought from Thinis, mixed with cumin and dried onions and a little of the pool's water, in the hot sand by the fire, but not too close to the heat, so the pot wouldn't crack. The sand warriors contributed to the feast too, with a hare and a hyena that they'd speared earlier that day.

It was the first time Narmer had ever eaten hyena. The meat was bitter, and he had to force himself to pretend it was delicious.

The Trader smiled at him across the glowing camel droppings. 'The People of the Sand believe that hyena meat is good for aching joints.'

'Is it?'

'Perhaps.'

'How do they live in this wilderness?' murmured Narmer. 'Just sand and puddles of water . . .'

The Trader raised an eyebrow. 'They are your enemies yet you don't know how they live?'

Narmer flushed.

'They live as most people live,' said the Trader. 'But it takes more land for them to do it. You hunt in a small space by the River. They hunt from waterhole to waterhole. They pick dates at one spot, and manna from the tamarinds in another . . .'

'Manna?'

'Tiny animals suck the sap from the trees, and give out a thick white honey on the trees every morning in midsummer. The People of the Sand have learnt to read the desert. They follow foxes or hares or pigeons to water. When the rains come, the jackals and hyenas lead them to high ground away from the floods.'

Narmer watched the men across the fire, chewing the hyena bones they held in their left hands and scooping up the barley mash with the fingers of their right hands. 'Why do they attack Thinis, then, if they have such a good life in the desert?'

'Because their world is growing drier,' replied the Trader. 'Springs that gave water a year ago are empty now.'

'How do you know all this?' asked Narmer. 'Nitho said you had never met these people before!'

'But I have met other People of the Sand,' said the Trader calmly. 'And people who have met the People of the Sand. The world has more links than you may have guessed.'

The People of the Sand wrapped themselves in their camel-skin cloaks that night to sleep. But Narmer stayed awake. The Trader had said that it was a tradition of the People of the Sand that any man they had eaten with was a friend, yet Narmer still preferred to stay on guard.

In the end nothing happened. The strangers left before dawn, taking their precious ointment with them, striding off into the desert as though it were as familiar to them as the Royal Courtyard back home was to Narmer — which he supposed in a way it was. For a moment he wondered where they were headed, who they were planning to attack. To another oasis, like this one, but with children playing by the water? Or even to join with others and raid Thinis? But there was nothing he could do about it now.

Nitho called out to Bast, who had kept her distance from the oasis. Narmer had been grateful for it: one of them might have speared her in terror — or, worse, the cat might have attacked them.

Narmer watched as Nitho hugged the great animal and gave her a bird she'd snared at the pool. And then they too left, heading southeast across the desert.

CHAPTER 14

The days passed slowly, days of sand and heat. They brought growing satisfaction for Narmer. For at last the Trader began to talk to him, sometimes striding beside his chair, or sitting beside him in the quiet of the night before the fire.

Had the Trader been waiting for Narmer to learn Sumerian? Or had Narmer passed some kind of test when he bargained with the Sand People? Whichever it was, Narmer drank in the new knowledge as though it were cool water from a spring.

The Trader used the sun to guide them, it seemed, and now before they slept each night he showed Narmer how to use the stars for guidance too, while the cat purred on Nitho's feet and the guards snored. The Trader explained how a traveller must keep looking behind him, so he'd remember what the view looked like in that direction, in case he ever needed to return.

There were other lessons too, like how to watch the way the land rose and fell, to work out where water might be seeping. There were stories about strange lands and even stranger people, which Narmer realised were meant to teach as well as entertain, like the tale of the afreet at that long-ago feast back in Thinis.

Each day his walking grew easier. His feet toughened and became calloused by the hot sand. His face and hands darkened to the colour of a bread crust, and his cheeks lost their softness.

Hunger gnawed at him like a jackal with fresh bones, not for food — their supplies were enough to keep them fed — but for familiar food, cucumbers and radishes and catfish.

And then the sand wind came.

It started as a red haze, spreading across the dawn horizon soon after they left camp. The Trader noticed it first. He muttered something to the others, too fast for Narmer to understand the Sumerian.

Narmer had been limping along, proud of how well he could walk now. But suddenly the Trader barked an order. The porters put down the chair for him to climb onto.

'What's wrong?' he asked Nitho.

'Look at the sky,' she said abruptly. 'Get on the chair. Hurry! The porters can carry you much faster than you can walk.'

The porters lifted his chair and broke into a jog.

Narmer looked where Nitho had pointed. 'A sandstorm,' he observed. He was used to sandstorms at home: hours or days when the sky wept sand that crept into every crevice, so that the women had to spend days sweeping it from floors and pathways. It was going to be uncomfortable being in one out here, he thought, without any shelter but the tents. 'But why are we hurrying?'

Nitho didn't look at him. Her face seemed blank, as though there were no time for emotion now. All her strength now seemed to be caught in keeping up with the porters and the Trader with her limping stride. 'Because if we are caught in it, we die.'

The first gusts of sand were stinging their eyes when they came to a rock.

It wasn't a very big rock. It poked out of the endless flat land as though a giant bird had been carrying it and had dropped it among the sand. But the others seemed to welcome it as though it were a palace with open doors.

The porters began to put up the biggest of the tents in the side of the rock that would be sheltered from the wind. But this time they tied all the tent poles except one together to make one long pole, then draped the tent skins over them. The narrow, too-tall tent looked weird to Narmer, but he didn't want to interrupt them with questions. At last they hammered a final pole into the sand next to the tent, and tied half the baggage onto it.

'Inside,' ordered the Trader briefly.

Narmer crawled into the tent. There was just enough room for all of them to crouch together with the rest of the luggage. Even the cat was crammed half onto Nitho's lap and half onto his.

Had Narmer ever sat with other people crowded about him like this? Smelling their breath, their sweat? Not that he could remember. No one crowded a prince. But he was a prince no longer. And out here, he realised, the desert didn't care who was king and who was commoner.

Then the wind hit them.

Suddenly Narmer understood the full truth of Nitho's words. The hills of Thinis protected it from the full force of the sandstorms that raged across the desert. But out here the wind meant death.

'If you were outside the tent,' said the Trader, his voice pitched high over the growl around them, 'the wind would eat the flesh from your bones. Or it would suffocate you, bury you in sand. Your body would dry in its sandhill till the end of time.'

'But we're safe in the tent?'

'No,' said the Trader. 'But we may survive.'

That day passed in a blur for Narmer. One day? Or was it more? The wind yelled about the tent. The sand lashed and buffeted. At times it seemed as though the sand were a living thing, prowling round the tent, trying to feast on the puny humans inside.

Together they held down the edges of the tent against the tugging of the wind. And then there was no need to hold it down, for the sand outside held it down instead.

The heat was unbearable. But the unbearable still has to be borne. The air grew stale, stinking of sweat and fear and cat. Even in the desert's dryness it turned moist and clammy from their breath.

And now there was a new danger. For as the sand about them grew higher it threatened to collapse their tent. They could only press their backs against the goatskin, gulping mouthfuls of water in the fetid darkness, bumping at each other's limbs, or the cat's, pinching each other to keep themselves awake so they would keep pushing against the sand that was trying to drown them.

Narmer's mouth grew dry, as though the wind and sand were sucking every scrap of moisture from his body. His tongue swelled. His lips cracked. His skin felt like old leather left out in the sun to dry.

And the beast outside kept screaming.

An endless nightmare later, Narmer felt Nid try to stand. He seemed to be lifting a pole upwards.

'What is it?' Narmer's tongue was so swollen that the words were slurred.

'Too much sand on top of us,' muttered Nid, 'blocking the air hole at the top. Without air we die.' He moved the pole again. 'I'm trying to clear the blockage.'

Did it work? Narmer supposed it must have. Because he kept on breathing, kept on living ...

He must have slept, sitting upright, crammed against the others. Or perhaps time just blurred to nothing.

And finally, so gradually it was hard to say when it happened, the wind began to die away.

Narmer glanced at Nitho. He could just make out her eyes in the dimness, but he caught the movement as she nodded.

'The storm is easing,' said the Trader hoarsely.

'How long ...' Narmer's voice ended in a croak.

'Soon,' answered the Trader.

He was right. With each passing moment the sound of the wind grew quieter, as though it were a desert animal that had simply walked away.

The Trader passed the water bag around again, as though to celebrate. Narmer felt the warm water soothe the dry ache in his throat. It was almost as if he could feel it flooding into the dry, cramped reaches of his body.

And at last there was silence, broken only by their breathing and a hiss from Bast. A heavier, denser silence than Narmer had even known.

'Time to leave,' said the Trader softly. 'If we can. No, stay still,' he told Narmer, who was about to move. 'The sand can still kill us.'

Nid and Portho rose and stood together, their backs still pressed against the goatskin to stop the sand from collapsing on them all. Then slowly, very slowly, Nid climbed up on Portho's shoulders. He pushed at the roof of the tent to open it.

A wave of sand slithered down on top of them. Narmer choked, instinctively shutting his eyes. Bast hissed. Sand ... and more sand ... around Narmer's feet, his legs, up to his waist ...

And then it stopped. And when Narmer looked up again, there was the sky, high and still, blue and safe above them, as Nid and Portho pushed through the sandhill around them to force a way out.

They had survived.

CHAPTER 15

Bast leapt out next, climbing over the humans with her rough paws as though they were a convenient set of mountains to scale. Nitho and the Trader climbed out after her. Portho leant down and helped Narmer clamber awkwardly up the piled sand and out of the tent. The fresh air was sweet as honey, soft as milk.

He grinned at Nitho. But she wasn't looking at him. She and the others were frantically digging down into the sand where they had left their luggage.

Narmer looked around him in disbelief. The rock they'd camped by had vanished. How had so much been carried off by the wind?

He limped over to help them, while the cat shook herself and began to wash.

At least the sand was easy to shift. But there was no sign of the pole that held down their baggage. For a moment Narmer wondered if they were digging in the right place, but then Nid's hands uncovered a piece of broken wood. The pole had snapped in the wind.

No one said anything. They redoubled their efforts, pushing and heaving at the sand. Suddenly Nitho gave a cry. There were the two large packs, still safe in their goat hide, tied to the bottom of the pole. But the smaller pack that the Trader had carried was gone.

Narmer sat back. 'Not much lost.' Then he saw the expressions of the others. 'What's wrong?'

'The small pack contained the gold,' said Nitho briefly.

'But . . . but can't we find it?'

Nitho gestured at the sand, which continued unbroken to the horizon. 'Where? It must have been blown away when the pole snapped. It could be anywhere. We might dig all our lives and it would still be lost.'

Narmer stared at her, then at the Trader. What did this mean? What happened to traders who had nothing to trade? Poor people in Thinis lived on what they could glean from others' fields, hunting for fallen grain on the ground, begging and living on dried fish and papyrus stems. It had never occurred to him that one day he might be poor too.

'Don't you have gold at home?' he asked hopefully.

'No,' said the Trader briefly. 'A trader's wealth is in the goods he carries. We carried riches to Thinis, and left with more riches: the gold. Now we have none.'

No one said anything. Narmer gazed at the world of sand about him. What had he done? Left a life of comfort for poverty . . . starvation?

And then he looked over at Nitho. She seemed concerned, but not devastated. Nor were the porters beating their chests in despair.

Bast yawned, and nosed curiously at one of the packs.

The Trader gazed into the desert, lost in thought. Finally he turned back to Narmer and Nitho, and smiled.

'So,' he said, 'Thinis's gold was not the fortune that the Oracle said I'd find. But we can still trade in Punt.'

'How?' demanded Narmer. '... Sir,' he added.

'The Queen does all Punt's trading herself. I have traded with her many times. She will trust me, I think. She'll loan us myrrh to trade for copper and turquoise in Ka'naan, knowing we will repay her. We won't make the fortune on this trip that I hoped.' His smile grew wider. 'But it could be worse. We have water, and grain enough to feed us and to pay our way to Punt. And even better ...'

'What?' asked Narmer.

The Trader's dark eyes looked at him from their pillows of wrinkles. 'We are alive.'

And finally they came to the sea.

Narmer had heard of the sea. Travellers called it 'the Great Blue'. But he'd never quite believed in it. Water that stretched to the horizon ...

But now that he was here it was strangely disappointing. It wasn't blue at all, more a sort of rippling greenish grey. And the shore was barren, despite all the water. He had expected to walk from desert into greenery, just like back home, where you walked from the red desert to the black moist soil that supported plants and birds and towns.

But here the desert stretched right down to the water, apart from a few cubits of rocky beach along the edge. The only signs of greenery were a cluster of palms and tamarisk trees near a huddle of stone huts, which looked as if someone had just piled rocks together and hoped that they'd give shelter.

Nitho saw the expression on his face and laughed up at him in his chair. 'What were you expecting? Another Thinis? There aren't any big towns along this coast!'

Narmer flushed. 'Why don't the people here grow things with all this water? They don't even have a patch of onions!'

'Because it's salt,' said Nitho matter-of-factly. 'Didn't you know that the seas are salt?'

'Salt?'

'Taste it,' said the Trader calmly, watching Narmer with a small smile on his face.

The porters lowered Narmer's chair. He forced himself to his feet and limped awkwardly down to the water. He took a mouthful of seawater and immediately spat it out. 'It's disgusting! Not even fish could live in this!'

'They do, you know,' the Trader told him. 'But they're different sorts of fish from the ones in your river. Salt water won't grow plants either, nor can animals drink it.'

'Then what do the people here drink?'

'There's a freshwater spring by those rocks. That's why they built their houses here. They live on fish and dates, and people pay them to use their boats.'

Narmer put his hand up to shield his eyes from the sea's glare and searched the horizon. 'Which boats?'

'The men are out fishing now,' explained Nitho. 'But when they come in we'll ask them to sail to Punt to ask a captain to bring a ship here to pick us up.'

'Why can't we go in their fishing boats?'

'Because they have only two or three small boats here. They'd have to make several trips to fit us all in, with our baggage too. But a large ship from Punt can carry us all.'

Ships that could carry thirty men ... Narmer remembered when Nitho had first told him of such big ships. It seemed like a lifetime ago. 'Why do we have to go by ship at all? Why can't we just keep walking down to Punt?'

The Trader and Nitho exchanged a glance. Narmer hated it when they did that. It made him feel ignorant, and an outsider.

'The Nubian lands are just south of here,' explained the Trader, gesturing to the porters to set the tents up further down the shore.

'The Nubians don't like traders?'

The Trader shrugged. 'Sometimes they do, sometimes they don't. When they do you come away with lion skins and gold.'

'And when they don't?'

'Then you never come away at all,' said the Trader matter-of-factly. 'I've only been to Nubia once,' he added. 'That was enough.'

Narmer and Nitho sat on the shore in the thin, shifting shade of the palm trees as Jod and Nid set up the tents in the shelter of the rocks, while Portho hunted for driftwood for one of his small, fast fires. The women in the huts looked out cautiously, then, recognising the Trader's party, gave them grilled fish and fresh dates in return for some of the barley the travellers had brought from Thinis.

The Trader propped his head on a bundle and dozed, and so did Bast, her head on Nitho's lap. The women peered at the cat nervously, as though they expected her to wake up and carry them off.

Narmer watched Nitho's hand idly rub the creature's tufted ears. It seemed impossible now that anyone would think those slender hands belonged to a boy.

'How will you get Bast onto the boat?' he asked suddenly.

Nitho shrugged. 'I won't. She'll come if she wants to. Every day we travel I wonder if it will be the day she decides to stay behind.'

'How old is she?'

The cat rolled slightly, allowing Nitho access to her fluffy stomach, and began to lick the salt from behind Nitho's knees with her rough tongue. Nitho shoved her head away. 'That tickles!' She turned back to Narmer. 'Not quite two summers. We were up in Ka'naan trading for copper when I found her.'

'Why do you want copper? It's too soft to be useful. It doesn't even keep its shine like gold.'

'Copper and tin together make bronze, and bronze is the hardest material there is. Spears tipped with bronze go further and cut cleaner than any tipped with stone.'

'Why didn't you bring bronze to Thinis, then?'

'We'd have had to carry the bronze all the way from Sumeria. It's heavy. Thinis isn't rich enough to make it worth carrying bronze all that way.'

Narmer's eyes were wide. 'But Thinis is the most powerful town in the world!'

'In *your* world,' said Nitho drily. 'Your *old* world.'

'But look around you!' Narmer gestured at the mean huts by the shore. How could Nitho possibly think that there was any other place like Thinis?

'Just wait,' said Nitho softly. 'You haven't seen anything yet, o great Prince Narmer.'

CHAPTER 16

The three tiny fishing boats came back at dusk. For the next six days the Trader's party camped by the edge of the sea, while one of the boats made the journey to Punt, to order a larger ship to call for them.

Narmer was glad of the rest. The hardships of the desert had hurt his leg more than he had expected, despite the ointment the Trader gave him to put on it.

It was good to rest in the shade of the trees, to have time to let his new way of life seep into him.

He had been watching the way the ripples shivered across the water one afternoon when Nitho sat down beside him. She put her chin on her knees and stared out at the sea too. 'I'm worried about our master,' she said abruptly.

Narmer glanced over to the huts, where the Trader was removing a splinter from the foot of one of the dusty children. 'Why?'

'He's different since we left Thinis. You wouldn't understand. You never knew him before.'

'Tell me anyway,' said Narmer.

'He's quieter. You noticed his silence too, remember?

I didn't think anything of it at first. But now … it's as though he's thinking about something he won't talk about.'

'Maybe he's homesick for Sumer.'

'Or ill.' Nitho cast another anxious glance back at the white-garbed man and the squirming, naked child.

But the Trader didn't seem sick to Narmer. He ate the bread that Nitho baked, the fish and dates the women gave them. He didn't have the cough either. But sometimes old people just faded away, like pomegranate leaves in winter.

What would happen to Nitho if their master died? Narmer wondered. Or to him? What other trader would take a scarred girl and a crippled youth? What if —

A movement caught his eye: a wading bird, of a type he'd never seen, come to stalk along the beach. Without thinking he grabbed the slingshot at his belt and a pebble from the ground, and let it fly. The bird dropped to the ground.

Narmer grinned. He might not be able to walk much, but his eye was as accurate as ever. He was just about to use his stick to clamber to his feet when Bast slunk out of the shadows by the rocks. She padded up to the dead bird, sniffed it, then took it in her jaws.

Narmer laughed. 'I thought we might have meat for dinner. But it looks like the bird is Bast's dinner instead.'

The cat hesitated. Then slowly she began to walk towards them. But this time she passed Nitho and laid the bird at Narmer's feet. She seemed to be waiting for him to do something.

'She realises you were the one who killed it!' breathed Nitho. 'It's your bird, not hers! I've never known her to do that before.'

Narmer looked at the great cat, watching him silently through her slanted eyes. He was tempted just to give the whole bird to her. But something stopped him. He took his flint knife from his belt and sawed off the bird's head, then gutted the body swiftly. He held out the head and guts to the cat.

Bast bent her furry head and took them from his hand, then padded back to sit by Nitho and enjoy them.

Nitho gazed at the cat, and then at Narmer. 'That's incredible!' she said.

Narmer grinned. He thought it was incredible too. It was good to have someone think he was special again.

Even if it was only the cat.

The fishing boat returned on the evening of the sixth day. But it was not alone.

Narmer stared — then caught Nitho looking at him with amusement, and flushed. He could just imagine what she was thinking.

This massive craft was bigger than any boat he'd dreamed of back in Thinis. It was made of wood, not bundles of reeds tied together like the fishing boats and other vessels at home. It was at least forty cubits long and comfortably wide as well, with a deck made of wood above an empty space for storing cargo. There were bench seats at the front and back and even a shelter on deck like a tent, to keep off the sun and rain.

The sails were massive, and there were oars for the half dozen rowers who crewed the ship, for it seemed that this big sea was too deep for a pole. It had a strange thing called a rudder at one end that somehow turned the ship in the direction it needed to go.

Narmer watched it, fascinated. Ships like this could carry all sorts of things up and down the River, he thought. Even stone and cedar wood. One town could make things the others needed and —

He closed his mind to the thought. Thinis was in his past. It was time he stopped thinking like its prince.

The ship pulled in next to a big clump of rocks, where the water was deep enough to float her safely. The sailors fastened a thick rope to a wooden stake hammered into the ground, then threw a plank over to the shore.

A tall man walked across it. He was dressed like the porters, in a kilt of leopard skin. His skin was dark like theirs too, and hairless as a girl's, except for a beard like the Trader's, short and trimmed with no moustache, though Narmer was sure that this beard was not held on with string. He wore jewellery as well, thick bands of some dark metal on his wrists and ankles, and his belt buckle was made of the same material. He asked Nitho what it was.

'That's the bronze I told you about,' she replied. She had pulled up her scarf again and spoke in her boy's voice, even though the man was too far away to hear her voice. 'He's the Captain.'

The man yelled something and came towards them. Evidently he and the Trader were old friends, for they clapped each other on the back and began to talk in Sumerian, without the need of a translator.

Narmer watched them. The Trader looked fine to him, no sign of illness or weakness either. Surely there could be nothing seriously wrong.

It took less time than Narmer had thought to stow the luggage under the deck. After that they all clambered aboard. Finally Bast, who had been washing herself by the palm trees and looking as though she hadn't even noticed the ship, gave her whiskers one last rub, rose, stretched and casually stalked over the plank too, her tufted tail waving. She made her way to the tent skins piled on the deck, pummelled them three times with her paws, then lay down as though all the preparation had been simply to make her a comfortable bed.

Narmer caught Nitho's eye and smiled. He was surprised to find how relieved he was that the cat had come aboard.

Sailing on a ship was not like sailing on the River, Narmer discovered. The ship rocked even more than being carried on a chair by the porters. It was enough to make him queasy — but not quite enough to make him throw up over the side in front of Nitho.

He had wondered how she would pretend to be a boy on the ship. But it seemed that she and the Trader shared the shelter at night, with the curtain pulled down for privacy. The Trader used a chamber pot, instead of aiming overboard like the guards and sailors, so when Nitho did the same no one took it for anything except eccentricity.

In fact the journey was hardest of all on Narmer. The deck swayed and shuddered so much it was impossible to stay upright with only one good leg. He was glad that there was nothing for him to do but doze and watch the shore pass by or the sailors grilling the fish they'd caught on their small charcoal fire in the prow.

Bast, it seemed, liked fish as well. It was a brave sailor who kept a fish that a wildcat had her eye on. But mostly she was content with eating the heads and guts, and sleeping on the goatskins or the most comfortable of the seats, but somehow always with her head towards Nitho, as though even dozing she needed to keep her mistress in view.

They sailed for two days and two nights. Narmer was worried, at first, when the ship kept moving even in the dark. But it seemed that the captain knew the way. And on the third day they came to Punt.

CHAPTER 17

The Season of Harvest (Summer)

Narmer thought it was a hill at first — whiter than the sand, gleaming distantly in the sunrise. But as the ship sailed closer he realised that it wasn't a hill at all.

'The Queen's palace,' said Nitho softly, coming to stand next to him at the prow. She had changed into women's dress, with a longer skirt, and bracelets on her wrists and over the scars on her ankles. 'The most beautiful palace in the world.'

Narmer felt excitement wash through him. 'What about their king?'

'Punt is always ruled by a queen. She has husbands sometimes, but they never become king.'

Narmer frowned. 'A land must have a king. Who else can lead the army and protect the people?'

Nitho laughed. Bast looked up at the sound, decided it was nothing to worry about, and put her head on her paws again. 'Punt's wealth is its myrrh trees. It's the women who know how to collect the sap and purify it. If strangers attacked I think the women might just forget how to tap the trees.'

'The invaders could steal the trees. Grow them somewhere else.'

Nitho shook her head. 'The trees only grow on the hills of Punt. My master tried to grow them back in Sumer, oh, years ago. But the trees always die. No, the Queen will rule as long as the trees give their sap. And that will be forever.'

Narmer stared at the gleaming white dome across the water. 'I've never seen anything so white!'

'Alabaster. It's a type of stone.'

'I know what alabaster is. But I've never seen a whole building made of it.'

Nitho grinned. 'That's the Queen's palace. Punt is small, but it's famous for its wealth.'

'Just like Thinis,' said Narmer happily.

Nitho gave him a look that was hard to interpret. 'Not quite like Thinis,' she said. And refused to say any more.

No, thought Narmer, gazing down at the crowded dock from the deck of the ship. Punt wasn't like Thinis at all.

He had been proud of his town till now. Thinis was the biggest and most powerful of the towns along the River — well, arguably, at any rate. But in Punt even the docks were larger than the town of his birth.

Jetty after jetty of giant boulders speared out into the sea. At each one there were ships — ships like theirs, with big square sails; fishing boats, but bigger than any he'd ever seen; and other ships, with strange pointed prows. There were sailors with skins of every shade from milk to ebony, wearing brown kilts to their knee, or lion or leopard skins, or tunics like the Trader's. Others wore nothing but a loincloth, with bangles at their wrists and ankles.

Sailors bargained with women carrying trays of fresh bread, and offered them a curl of cinnamon bark or an ostrich feather in exchange for food that didn't taste of salt and sweat; a tumbler somersaulted in return for drinks; someone's monkey ran squeaking and screeching up a mast, while a mob of sailors argued about the best way to get it down.

And the women! They wore kilts, like men ... and their breasts were bare! Children were usually naked in Thinis, and men worked naked too. But women covered their chests.

Narmer stared, almost breathless with the newness of it all. It was noisy, confusing — and fascinating.

Suddenly he noticed Nitho and the Trader whispering together. Instead of excitement their faces showed worry and concern.

'What's wrong?'

'It's too quiet,' murmured Nitho.

'Quiet?' Narmer started to smirk, then stopped when he saw their faces. 'Look at it all!' He waved at the noise around them.

'You've never seen it before.' The Trader's voice was even quieter than Nitho's. 'All this is just the bustle of the docks. Look more closely. Nearly every ship is leaving. There are no porters from the palace carrying trade goods. Something's wrong.'

'It even smells wrong,' added Nitho.

Narmer sniffed the air. It *did* smell strange — a scent of smoke and spices. But he had assumed that was just what this land of myrrh always smelt like.

'The smell of burnt offerings,' said Nitho quietly. 'I wonder what all those people are praying for.'

The Trader looked around him, his face unreadable. 'I don't like it.'

Nid left Jod and Portho, who were guarding the baggage, and came over to them. 'The Captain said all was well when he left a few days ago. Whatever it is has happened since. What do you think, Master?'

The Trader gave a small shrug. 'It's not plague, or we'd hear the women wailing. It's not war, or there'd be soldiers.'

'Should we stay?'

The Trader considered. 'After what happened to our gold, we don't have much choice,' he said at last. 'But keep close together. Be prepared to leave as soon as I give the word.'

'So what do we do now?' asked Narmer.

'We head straight for the Queen's palace. They'll know what's happening, if anyone does. We'd better put on our best clothes first,' he added.

Narmer nodded. He wondered if he'd feel like a prince of Thinis again, in his good kilt and sandals. He doubted it. Thinis was another world now.

The porters shouldered the baggage. Nitho fixed a collar about the cat's neck and fastened a woven leather lead to it. Bast prowled at the side of Narmer's chair, as though she had been trained since kittenhood to follow her mistress through crowds like this.

Narmer felt embarrassed at being carried through the streets. But he still walked too slowly to keep up in a crowd.

As soon as they had left the docks he saw what Nitho had meant. The town was ... waiting, he decided. But even if the streets were quiet, Punt was still amazing.

Too many streets to count, and wide spaces filled with shops and market stalls, their counters piled high with carpets or rich fabrics, cooking pots or alabaster vases. And women everywhere — and all with naked breasts. Big breasts, small breasts. Narmer almost felt as if the breasts were staring at him.

But none of the women was fingering the shawls or rugs on the market stalls. Instead, they stood in clusters, whispering. Women sat in doorways, too, grinding grain in quirms, not gossiping or singing as they might at home, but silent, as though they watched for news.

Narmer had never imagined a town as quiet as this. Or a town as beautiful. Every building seemed to be painted or covered with tiles, so the whole scene was a clash of shapes and colours. Even the road was paved with small stones, to protect their feet from dust.

'What is that building?' he asked Nitho. 'The long one with all the columns.'

She looked in the direction he was pointing. 'It's the Temple of Inanna,' she said. 'She's the goddess of wisdom and war, and all growing things too.'

'Like Isis? What are all those women doing sitting outside it?'

Nitho flushed. 'They're waiting to make their offering.'

'But they're not carrying anything,' objected Narmer. 'What sort of offering are they making?'

Nitho almost looked embarrassed, Narmer thought. But Nitho was never embarrassed. 'The usual,' she said shortly.

'There are more women than I've ever seen at the Temple,' said the Trader. 'I wonder what they're asking the goddess for today.'

Narmer shook his head, puzzled. There was something else that was strange about this town, he thought. And suddenly he knew.

Where were all the men?

There had been men down at the docks, loading up their ships. There were a few men tending gardens too. But every shopkeeper seemed to be a woman. And so many women out in the streets too. The women of Punt, Narmer realised, ran a lot more than their households.

It was a strange idea. Back home women could own land, but decisions were made by their fathers or husbands. A woman rarely showed herself beyond the walls of her courtyard, except to wash clothes or gather greens or fallen grain.

Punt, it seemed, was different.

Nitho seemed different too, Narmer realised. Back in Thinis and on the ship she had been acting as a young man. But here she wore a girl's dress, and showed her face.

But right now she looked worried, and so did the Trader.

Narmer tried to think. What would happen if they had to leave here without anything to trade? He was beginning to realise how very little he knew about the Trader and the way of life he had committed to.

Narmer had heard of tribes down south who sold their young people into slavery when times were bad. What exactly was Narmer's status with the Trader? Could he too be sold if things got desperate?

Back in Thinis he had assumed that the whole world was like the one he knew. He'd thought he could change from prince to trader in a day. But despite his talent for bargaining, he knew now that he was a long way from being a trader. He couldn't even walk properly, or carry baggage. Every one of the porters was more valuable than he was.

The palace towered above them as they grew closer, like a miniature mountain that some god had decided to make more beautiful than a natural hill could ever be. The porters stayed with the luggage while the Trader, Nitho, Narmer and the cat climbed the staircase to the palace.

Narmer had seen stairs before — there had been a set of steps leading up to the palace back in Thinis. But he had never seen as many stairs as these. It looked as though the stair makers had thought they might keep going to the sky. Even the columns above them were ten times the height of the tallest one at Thinis, smooth and perfect, the white rock dappled with lights from the sea.

He bit his lip as they climbed. Every stair was agony. But he tried not to let the pain show on his face.

A woman appeared as they neared the top of the stairs. For a moment Narmer thought she must be the Queen herself. She had gold at her throat and wrists, and was dressed in a tunic as white as the stone around her. It covered her dark brown shoulders but left her breasts bare.

But it seemed that she was just a servant. She recognised Nitho and bowed, then bowed to Bast, then a smaller bow to the Trader and finally, as an afterthought, a bob of the head to Narmer.

'I am sorry, mistress,' she said to Nitho in the Sumerian tongue. 'There will be no trading done today.'

Narmer blinked. It seemed that here in Punt a girl like Nitho was more important than a man.

'Why not?' demanded Nitho.

The woman glanced at the Trader and Narmer uncomfortably.

'We will wait for you down the stairs,' said the Trader quickly.

It was even harder walking back down. Narmer would have liked to ask the Trader to help him, but he was too embarrassed. 'Why can't we stay?' he asked instead.

The Trader glanced back to the top of the stairs, where Nitho and the woman were talking, with Bast sitting nearby, washing her face with one paw, as though she just happened to be passing and felt the need to groom herself. 'Women make the decisions here. I suspect that whatever has happened is women's business. The Queen's servant will speak more freely without us.'

Finally Nitho came back down the stairs with a grim look on her face. 'The Queen is dying.' She bit her lip. 'They say it might be any day now.'

So that explained the silence and the offerings at the Temple, thought Narmer. Of course no business would be done while the Queen was ill.

'We'll have to wait till the new queen is crowned then, won't we?' asked Narmer.

'No one is sure who the new queen will be,' said Nitho shortly. 'The Queen's daughters are still small children. The Queen has an aunt and a female cousin. Maybe one of them will become regent, or even seize the throne themselves. No one seems to know what will happen. But everyone is afraid.'

'Aunt or cousin, it makes little difference to us,' said the Trader quietly. 'I know neither of them. Neither is likely to advance us anything on trust.' He shook his head. 'I am sorry. Not for us, but for the Queen. She is a good woman, and a great ruler. Punt's riches could have tempted a dozen invaders, yet the Queen has kept the land safe.'

'How?' asked Narmer.

The Trader gave a half-smile. 'The Queen deals fairly with everyone. If anyone tried to invade they would feel the wrath of Punt's friends. No, she will be hard to replace.'

There seemed nothing to say. The travellers stood like a silent island in the midst of the street, with the Trader lost in thought.

Finally Narmer asked, 'What's wrong with the Queen? Is it an illness? She must still be young to have young daughters.'

'The servant just said that the Goddess has grasped her by the throat. She can hardly breathe.'

'Aha,' said the Trader softly. 'I think I know why.'

They stared at him. 'When I last saw her, half a year ago, there was a lump at her throat. I've seen something like it before, back in Sumer. It was a growth that pressed upon the breathing pipe. As it got bigger the man couldn't breathe.'

'Did he die?' asked Nid.

'The priests cut it out. One of them knew I was interested in such things, and let me watch. He lived.'

'Then you can save the Queen!' cried Narmer. 'Cut out the growth!'

The Trader began to laugh. 'Listen to the boy! Why do you think no one has tried that here?'

Narmer shook his head.

'One slip of the knife and the Queen would die. And anyone who touched her would be killed. Yes, and all their friends as well. Who do you think would take a risk like that?'

No one spoke. Then Narmer said, 'A man who faced an afreet and came away. Who conquered the desert and its storms. Who took a crippled boy and girl and let them live. A man like that would have the courage, I think.'

The silence grew. Narmer began to wonder if he had said too much and offended his master. It was hard to remember, sometimes, that he was not a prince who could take charge.

Then Nitho said, 'It's impossible. Isn't it?'

'No,' said the Trader at last. He didn't sound offended, Narmer realised with relief. Just thoughtful.

'It's not impossible. When you think about it, it is just another trade. We risk our lives. And in return . . .' The Trader hesitated. 'The Queen is a great ruler,' he said at last. 'Many envy Punt its riches, but the Queen has kept the kingdom secure. She doesn't deserve a death spent struggling for every breath.' He looked up towards the palace. 'We can try.'

CHAPTER 18

The servant came out again as they reached the top of the stairs. She seemed surprised to see them, and annoyed too.

'I told you . . .' she began.

Suddenly Nitho's voice was the Oracle's again, full of calmness and authority. 'The Goddess sent us. We have come to save the Queen.'

'To save her?' The servant hesitated. 'I am sorry,' she said at last. 'My orders are to admit no one.'

'Not even the people who will save your queen?' demanded Nitho.

'Tell Her Majesty that the Sumerian Trader would speak to her,' said the Trader quietly, 'that we have come to give her the breath she struggles for.'

'I don't know . . .' began the woman.

'Please do it,' said Nitho calmly.

The servant shrugged. 'I will try,' she said at last. 'But I don't know if anyone will listen.'

She left, and they waited under the colonnades. The scent of spices was thicker here and the air was greasy with smoke. The whole palace must be burning sacrifices for the Queen's recovery, thought Narmer.

'Well, Trader? Why do you interrupt our grief?'

The servant was back, bowing so low that her face touched the tiled floor. Two male servants, with bare feet and leopard-skin loincloths, prostrated themselves too. But none of them had spoken those words; it was another woman, who now walked slowly towards the travellers.

She was the fattest woman Narmer had ever seen, and one of the tallest too. Her flesh rolled as she walked. Her bare breasts were like the buckets that the gardeners at Thinis used to water their leeks. Narmer tried not to stare at them. Her ankle bracelets would have made a belt for anyone else. There were rings on her toes, and her heels and hands were decorated with swirls of red and orange. Her hair was long and thin, and a strange bright orange as well, piled onto her head and kept in place by another band of gold.

The woman glared at Nitho and the Trader.

'Well, Trader?' she demanded again, in strangely accented Sumerian. 'Why do you demand to see my royal niece at a time like this?'

Nitho bowed low, and so did the Trader. Narmer hurriedly copied them. This must be the Queen's aunt, he realised.

'We come to serve the Queen,' said the Trader, his face still towards the floor.

'So I have been told.'

Narmer felt, rather than saw, the Queen's aunt stare haughtily down at them. Did this woman really want to

125

save her niece? Perhaps she would rather see her niece dead, and herself in power.

But then the woman said, 'Her Majesty had a dream that someone would come across the sea to save her. It was a true dream, she thought. I have told Her Majesty that you are here. She wants to see you. I advised against it. The last thing she needs is strangers bothering her. But while she lives, her word is law. Come.'

The royal aunt walked in front, her fat buttocks wobbling under her kilt, with the cat stalking on her lead beside her, as though Bast had decided that cats were royalty too. Perhaps they *were* in Punt, thought Narmer, remembering how the servant had bowed to Bast. Through colonnades with courtyards on each side, each adorned with different flowers or fruits or fountains, and each as perfect as the last. Polished stone shone under their feet.

Narmer had thought the palace at Thinis was the most beautiful building in the world. But it was like a goatskin tent compared with this.

What sort of woman commanded beauty like this? he wondered, as he forced his leg to keep up with the others. Surely she must be lovely too.

'What's she like?' he whispered to Nitho.

'Shh. You mean the Queen?'

'Yes. Is she as beautiful as her palace?'

Nitho blushed, so her scars showed white against her face. 'She is a great woman, and a wise queen.'

'But is she beautiful?'

'Shh!' said Nitho again. She sounded angry. 'We're nearly there!'

A pair of wooden doors rose before them, the biggest and most ornately carved that Narmer had ever seen. He had seen doors before, of course — both the town and palace walls at home had outside doors that could be shut to keep out enemies. But he had never seen doors used inside, simply for privacy.

Two sentries stood on either side — women, not men, dressed in leopard-skin skirts, with two spears in either hand. They bowed to the aunt, nodded respectfully to Nitho, then unbolted the doors and pushed them open. The cat entered first, then Nitho, with the Trader and Narmer behind. The Queen's aunt hesitated in the doorway, then turned and left them, as though to say: *Whatever happens now has nothing to do with me!*

The massive doors closed behind her. Narmer hardly noticed. He was staring at the Queen.

She sat propped up by cushions on a throne, much more magnificent than the one back home. And this one was covered in gold.

Maybe the Queen had been beautiful, once. But now she was as thin as a desert mouse, and very frail. Even her hair was faded, rusty instead of black, and her eyes were shadowed. Worst of all was the giant lump that disfigured her neck, like a small monkey clamped under her flesh.

'Greetings, Trader, and Nitho,' said the Queen in passable Sumerian. Her voice was thin and husky. 'It is good to see old friends again.'

'I would like to say it is good to see you, Your Majesty,' said the Trader. 'But not as you are now. Would you permit me to look at the growth on your neck?'

The Queen laughed, but even that was hoarse and breathless. 'No "O glorious Queen, your radiant beauty shakes the world." Just "Can I take a look at your lump?" You used to be so good at flattery.'

'I am not sure Your Majesty has time for compliments,' said the Trader bluntly.

'I think you are right.' The Queen had to gasp for air even to finish her words. 'I dreamed of you, you know. I dreamed you'd save me. Approach me, then. I give you permission to touch my throat.'

The Trader bowed, then stepped forward and ran his hands over the Queen's neck. 'How fast has it grown?'

'It's doubled this last moon.'

'If it grows much more it will stop your breathing entirely,' said the Trader flatly, sitting back on his heels in front of her.

'I know.' She paused. 'Well? You told the servant you had come to save me. Are you going to do it?'

The Trader regarded her for a moment. 'Your Majesty, in all honesty, I do not know if I can help you.'

'You can't remove the lump?'

'Yes. I can do that. But I do not know if you will be alive afterwards.'

The Queen reached out and touched his hand. 'From one old friend to another,' she said hoarsely, 'please help me. When I heard that you had come I felt hope leap like a spring hare in my heart.'

The Trader didn't move. He seemed to be thinking. Finally he said, 'If you die after I've touched you I will be killed too, even if you give orders that I'm not to be harmed.

I'd risk that myself — from one friend to another, as you said. But I can't risk it for the children.' He gestured to Nitho and Narmer. 'Give them and my porters provisions and a three-day start back to Sumer. Then I will cut away the growth.'

'Thank you, old friend —' began the Queen, just as Nitho broke in.

'No!'

The Queen stared. She had probably never been interrupted before, Narmer supposed. Then she smiled.

'No?'

'No,' repeated Nitho. 'If my master stays, I stay. He is my friend as well as my master. I won't leave without him.'

'And as one new friend to another new friend,' said Narmer, 'I'm not leaving without Nitho. Or my master.'

'You see how they rule me?' said the Trader. 'An old man should be given respect, not arguments.'

'I'm not arguing,' said Nitho. 'I'm telling you, that's all.'

'*Mmrrow*,' said Bast. For a moment Narmer wondered if she was refusing to leave too. Then he realised that she had found a leopard kitten in a basket of cushions by the throne, and was mewing at it curiously.

But the noise had lightened the moment. The Trader stood up. 'When?' he asked.

'Now,' said the Queen quietly. 'Before I have time to be afraid.'

The Queen summoned her Council — the oldest women of each of Punt's main families — while the Trader made his preparations. Sharp obsidian knives were brought, bandages of linen scraped thin and smooth, an obsidian needle threaded with catgut. A wash of desert lavender and wormwood, a pot of honey, another pot of the ointment they had given to the People of the Sand ...

'May I help too?' asked Narmer quietly, as Nitho and the Trader discussed which of the knives had the thinnest, sharpest blade.

The Trader pulled the catgut to make sure it had no tears or weak points. 'Will you faint at the sight of blood?'

'No!'

'Then you can help,' he agreed — then added, as Narmer's eyes lit up, 'by keeping the cat out of the way as we work.'

'But ...' Narmer stopped. He had been going to say that he could do more than hold a wildcat. But could he? He knew nothing of healing. At least he would be with them as they worked.

The women of the Council had finished arguing — it seemed that each of them was quite confident enough to argue with a queen. But even though Narmer couldn't understand their speech, their tone and gestures made it clear that none seemed really opposed to the operation. Probably, thought Narmer, they were secretly glad that strangers were attempting it, and the matter had been taken out of their hands.

At last the women left. The doors were closed. The Trader had refused to have any witnesses. 'If she lives we will be heroes. If she dies we will be killed,' he said. 'No number of witnesses to say that we did our best will make any difference — except maybe to jolt my hand at the wrong moment.'

The Queen still reclined on her throne, wearing her crown, but now her eyes were closed. She muttered under her breath. Praying, thought Narmer. He imagined that the priests in every temple were praying too — or perhaps Punt only had priestesses …

'Your Majesty, if you would lie on the couch …' began the Trader.

The Queen opened her eyes. 'I will die as I live. A queen on my throne. Begin,' she ordered hoarsely.

Narmer shivered. He had seen warriors face battle, but none had shown such bravery as this.

Nitho held a cup up to her lips. 'Poppy,' she said. 'Enough to dull the pain, but not put you to sleep. The lump is so big it might stop your breathing if you slept.'

The Queen nodded. 'I no longer sleep,' she said wryly, 'just doze, then wake as I begin to choke.' She made a face at the bitter taste of the poppy.

'Tell me when the room turns misty,' said the Trader softly.

They waited. And then the Queen nodded.

Narmer grabbed the cat's collar and began to scratch her about the ears. He had discovered that she would sit still for any length of time if her ears were scratched. Bast subsided next to him and started to purr.

The Trader placed a towel around the Queen's neck then picked up the knife. 'Be as still as you can,' he whispered.

'I know.' The Queen's voice was drowsy. 'One slip and I am dead.'

Narmer shuddered. The memory of his own pain and struggle to live was too recent. But at least for him those days had been clouded by sleep.

The Trader began to cut. The Queen gave a strangled noise and her fingers tightened on the throne. But other than that she didn't move.

Bast's nostrils twitched at the smell of blood, but she stayed where she was.

It was like a nightmare, impossibly vivid, as though each moment were stretched out to an hour. Blood dripped from the Trader's hands and onto the towel, but it didn't spurt, as it did when an animal's throat was cut. The Trader had cut shallowly, just under the skin, avoiding the deeper veins and arteries.

I remember that smell, thought Narmer. The scent of human blood, so different from the blood of a sheep or deer. He felt helpless, sitting with his arms around the cat. How could the Queen bear it?

Suddenly he understood: the Queen bore all this for Punt, not for herself. For a moment he wished his father could meet this queen.

Then the Trader widened the cut, pulling the loose skin of her throat tight so he could slice more accurately. Nitho took a soft cloth and began to dab the blood away, so the Trader could see where to cut the Queen's flesh. He frowned in concentration. Sweat rolled down his forehead. Nitho's brown hands moved swiftly to wipe it away from his eyes with her cloth, leaving a smudge of the Queen's blood on his cheek.

The Queen made a noise, halfway between a groan and a gasp. Her feet twitched. But by some superhuman effort she kept the rest of herself still.

There was so much blood ... The stench of flesh was

everywhere. Bast gave a hiss, her eyes bright, as though the smell excited her.

Something fat and yellow plopped into the bucket by the throne. Narmer gasped.

More blood dripped onto the floor. Nitho handed the Trader the needle and catgut. Her hands trembled slightly, then steadied as she held the edges of the wound together while the Trader stitched. Now his forehead was drenched in sweat.

'Is she . . .' began Narmer.

'She is still alive,' said Nitho. 'But the operation isn't over yet.'

A spurt of blood hit Nitho's face and began to drip. Narmer felt the room begin to spin. He felt cold and hot at the same time. His stomach lurched.

Suddenly the bleeding stopped, as though a spring had been plugged by a stone. The Queen's head slumped forward.

Narmer felt terror grab his chest and squeeze. Was she dead? Had they killed her?

'Quickly!' the Trader gasped. Narmer stumbled forward as the Trader beckoned. 'She's fainted! Hold her head up or she'll choke!'

Narmer grasped the lolling head. The Queen's mouth was open and there was spittle at the corners. Her crown had slipped. Narmer ignored his instinct to straighten it. He glanced down. There was blood everywhere. His fingers were already slippery with it. Nitho's cloth was soaked, and her arms stained to the elbows. Fresh, bright red blood, and darker blood clots. But there was also a neat line of tiny stitches across the Queen's neck. And she still breathed.

'*Mrrow?*' To Narmer's horror the cat was nosing at the bucket. Nitho pushed her away with her foot. Bast glared at her, then retreated, peering at the basket where the leopard cub was sleeping through it all.

'Lie her down,' said the Trader, panting. 'Remember we have to keep her neck steady.'

He sounded as though he had run across the desert. Nitho's face, too, was white and running with sweat.

'But she said —' began Narmer.

'Do it!' he ordered.

Narmer had never heard the usually placid Trader speak like this before. He took the Queen's legs, as the Trader took her arms, while Nitho held her head. They carried her as gently as possible to the couch, and laid her flat, then Nitho arranged cushions to keep her head still.

The Queen was breathing in shallow gasps.

'Will she live?' whispered Narmer.

The Trader didn't reply. He held her wrist up to his ear. He put it down and shrugged. 'Wash her,' he instructed them tersely. 'Try to get rid of the blood.'

The attendants might panic if they saw a bloodstained Queen, thought Narmer. Trying not to gag, he picked up one of the unused linen bandages, dipped them in the scented water and washed the Queen's face, neck, her bare bosom, her arms and her hands, while Nitho wrapped up the bloody towels and moved the bucket of blood-stained water out of sight. When she looked up Narmer was startled to see tears in her eyes.

Then they waited. Narmer's heart was pounding. Would the Queen wake up?

Finally she groaned. Her eyes opened and she tried to move. The Trader jumped to his feet, his face flushed with relief. He dipped a clean cloth into the poppy juice, then gently held the Queen's chin while he squeezed the liquid into her mouth. 'You may sleep now, Your Majesty,' he said softly. 'The growth is gone! You have survived! Sleep, for as long as you need to, until the worst of the pain has disappeared.'

The Queen blinked at him with agony-blurred eyes. Her lips twitched in an almost smile. She swallowed with obvious effort, then swallowed again as the Trader dripped more juice into her mouth.

And then she slept.

CHAPTER 19

The afternoon shadows had lengthened outside the windows when a small door opened opposite the room's main entrance. Narmer wondered wearily what member of the Council had finally dared to enter the Queen's chamber uninvited.

But it was a small girl who peered in. 'Mama?'

Nitho got stiffly to her feet. She limped swiftly towards the child and took her in her arms. 'Your mama will live,' she told her.

'Will she?' The child stared at Nitho. 'Are you a queen too? No one is allowed to touch me unless they're royal.'

'She has helped save a queen,' said Narmer, smiling. 'That's almost as good as being a queen.'

Someone else looked around the door. It was a woman this time, one of the Queen's Council, her neck laden with pearls, her eyes smudged with fear. 'Is it true? Does the Queen live?'

'She lives,' said the Trader. His voice was unbearably tired, and Narmer saw that his hands were shaking.

'You need rest yourself,' said Nitho with concern, the princess still in her arms. 'We need somewhere nearby to sleep,' she told the woman, 'in case the Queen wakes up and needs us.'

The woman's eyes were wide with awe. 'Yes, Your ... Your Worthiness. Your rooms have been prepared.'

No one along the whole River had ever dreamed of luxury like this, thought Narmer, as he looked at the rich kilt laid out for him on the bed.

The room's ceiling was higher than that of any temple, the walls made from blocks of alabaster fitted so closely that the joins were impossible to see. The smooth stone floor was covered in finely woven carpets dyed a rainbow of colours. Splendid cloth hung on the walls, woven with scenes of birds, and leopards prancing through fields of flowers.

The bed was as big as his entire room at home, with carved lions instead of legs. Best of all was a giant bath, carried in on the shoulders of six male servants dressed in loincloths embroidered with fine gold. When Narmer felt the water it was as warm as fresh bread, and when he smelt it, it was as fragrant as his father's courtyard flowers.

Hot water merely to wash in!

He had just untied his filthy kilt when Nitho wandered in, with Bast following as though she had coincidentally decided to come the same way. The cat peered around the room in case there was food.

'Hey!' Narmer pulled his kilt back around his waist.

Nitho grinned. 'In Punt a woman goes where she wants to. The men do what they are told.'

'How is the Queen?'

'The master has just been to see her again. He gave her more poppy. But he says there's no more bleeding, and she's breathing well.'

'We did it!' said Narmer happily. '. . . Well, you and our master.'

'You helped too. I've sent for the porters. They'll be here soon.' She bit her lip. 'There may still be problems, you know. The wound will swell. She may get a fever — people often do, after things like this. But the master has put honey on the wound to sweeten it, and her women are holding damp cloths on it, scented with rose oil, to keep it cool and to keep the swelling down. He thinks she will be all right.'

Nitho looked almost like a stranger, Narmer thought in surprise. It wasn't just what she was wearing — a Punt-style kilt trimmed with gold, but with a shawl fringed in alabaster beads across her breasts and arms. Somehow she was walking like a woman now, as well as talking like one. The veiled 'boy' of Thinis and the desert was gone.

The fine clothes should have made her scar stand out even more. But the Trader had been right, Narmer realised. The scar was so familiar now that he hardly saw it. He just saw Nitho.

Nitho smiled. 'There's a meal for us in the courtyard.' She gestured to the patio beyond their rooms, with its view over the palace gardens and the city to the scrubby hills beyond. 'I'll see you out there soon,' she added.

Narmer finished untying his kilt. He slipped into the water and lowered himself into its silky embrace. The bath felt smooth and warm against his skin. A haze of perfume floated around him. The water relaxed muscles that ached from the tension of the operation.

He shut his eyes, then opened them when his stomach growled. The bath was all very well, but he needed food. He stepped out of the water, towelled himself, and fastened on the new kilt. It hung in soft rich folds against his legs.

There were combs and brushes laid out for him. He ran a comb through his hair and tied it with a leather thong, then slipped his feet into the sandals he had brought with him. He might be only an ex-prince from a small town on a distant river, but at least he knew enough not to go barefoot in a palace.

As he went out to join Nitho he caught a glimpse of a young man. He stopped and stared. The young man gazed back at him from a smooth brown sheet of metal hanging on the wall. He was good looking, Narmer thought, apart from a fading scar on one cheek, and bore himself proudly, as though he were . . .

A prince of Thinis, thought Narmer, suddenly recognising himself, but somehow older than he had imagined himself to be, his eyes bright in his desert-browned face. He had only ever seen his reflection in pools of water. But this polished bit of bronze reflected far better than water ever could. He ran his hand over it, but that was all it was: a thin, smooth disc. It must be just for showing people their reflections, he thought. What a peculiar idea.

He hobbled through colonnades carved into the shape of palm trees to reach the courtyard, where food had been spread out on a series of low tables. The air smelt sweet. The servants must have scattered scented oil onto the plants growing around the courtyard's edges, Narmer supposed, as bougainvillea had no scent.

There were three couches piled with cushions. Nitho and the Trader occupied two of them. The Trader looked different too. For the first time since Narmer had known him he had left off his false beard. His round chin was pinker than the rest of his face.

The third couch was occupied by the cat. She opened her eyes as Narmer approached, then quickly shut them again, carefully excluding him from any possibility of lying there himself.

He heard a muffled giggle from Nitho. She clapped her hands and a servant ran into the room.

'Another couch,' she ordered.

'At once, Your Worthiness.'

Narmer smiled. After the days of fear in the desert it was good to be treated with respect again. And somehow 'Worthiness' suited Nitho.

It was an extraordinary meal. Narmer had eaten well as a prince, but nothing like this. There were platters of small birds filled with grain and spices, stuffed cucumbers, fish made into small spiced balls and fried in oil, salads of finely chopped lettuce stems, leeks and pomegranate juice, and slices of a giant pink fruit with a thick white rind and green skin.

Narmer took a bite and felt the cold juice drip down his chin. It was probably the most delicious thing he'd ever tasted. 'What is this?' he asked.

'They call it watermelon,' said the Trader. 'The people in the deserts far to the south carry melons instead of water bags. The flesh is so cold because it is chilled with snow, brought from a mountain far to the south.'

'Snow?' The word was unfamiliar to Narmer. 'What's that?'

'Water. Very cold water that becomes solid.' The Trader selected another piece of melon. 'I have melons growing on my farm at home,' he added. 'I got the seeds from Punt.'

It was the first time the Trader had spoken of his home. What was it like? Narmer wondered. Not rich, perhaps; the Trader had said he had no gold at home. But somehow Narmer had assumed he owned a town house — like a baker, perhaps — not a farm.

Who was this man he was travelling with?

Suddenly a great cry sounded outside the courtyard walls. Narmer looked at Nitho and the Trader in alarm. The cry came again. But this time he realised that the sound was cheering.

Nitho clapped her hands to call one of the servants. A woman hurried in, bowing low. 'Yes, Your Worthiness?'

'What's happening?' Nitho asked her.

'The Council has given out the news,' the servant said. 'The Queen has spoken to her women.'

Nitho glanced at the Trader. He nodded, smiling. 'If she can speak, she will live.'

The servant's smile was as wide as a slice of watermelon. 'The Queen is saved!' She backed out of the room, still bowing.

'And so are we,' said the Trader, but softly, so that the servant didn't hear.

CHAPTER 20

The celebrations continued through the night. It was as though a fog had been lifted from the palace. Servants sang in the colonnades as they swept. The smell of smoke and spices was replaced by the scent of flowers. The women wore garlands on their heads and bosoms, hiding their breasts, for which Narmer was grateful. All that flesh was . . . interesting, but it was embarrassing trying not to stare at it.

Nothing was too good for the people who had saved Punt's beloved Queen. Fresh flowers were scattered through their rooms at dawn and dusk. Rose oil was sprinkled in front of them as they walked along the corridors. The best of everything was brought to them.

The Trader checked on the Queen throughout the following day. She was weak, but more at ease with her women and her daughters than with him. Within three days she was able to speak easily and sip soup instead of poppy, though her neck was still badly swollen around the wound.

On the fifteenth day the Trader took Nitho and Narmer with him while the cat stayed in their courtyard. Narmer watched as the Trader carefully cut the stitches and pulled out the catgut, and Nitho mopped the tiny traces of blood then wiped on ointment mixed with honey. The Queen flinched, and finally smiled.

'Why does a little pain like that seem harder to bear than the agony of your knives?'

The Trader smiled at her. 'Because you know that you will live. Now pain is an indignity, not a curse.'

'You have an answer for everything, old friend,' said the Queen. Her voice was regaining its strength too. 'Even this.' She touched her throat lightly. 'So, what does a queen offer in return for her life?'

Narmer half expected the Trader to say politely, 'Between friends no payment is needed.' But instead he stroked his bare chin where the beard had been. 'Whatever you think it is worth,' he replied, not even trying to hide his delight. Narmer had never seen him smile so broadly.

The Queen began to laugh, then stopped, as it hurt her bruised throat. 'Very well, my friend the trader. I offer all that you and your men can carry. Your choice of goods.'

The Trader's eyes gleamed. 'Your Majesty,' he said, 'you have fulfilled a trader's dream.'

It *was* like a dream, thought Narmer, as servant after servant brought in bales of panther skin, fragrant wood carved into delicate boxes, beads of lapis lazuli and turquoise, the bronze plates he now knew as mirrors, heaps of myrrh resin, slabs of ebony wood, piles of elephant tusks, small bowls filled with a strange, almost green-coloured gold, the rarest in the world, curls of cinnamon bark, khesyt wood, small coloured jars of incense, and eye cosmetics.

There were apes, too, and monkeys that chattered and tried to climb the wall hangings, and even a wild dog that had been tamed. The dog made Bast spit and her hackles rise, though she tolerated the apes and monkeys.

Narmer half hoped the Trader would let him take a monkey. But he agreed that the poor thing might die during the long trek through the dry lands to Sumer. Humans, it seemed, were tougher than monkeys.

Nor would the Trader take any of the slaves, even the most beautiful or strong, though he accepted the offer of more guards to go part of the way to Sumer with them.

Instead he chose nuggets of myrrh and bags of the greenish gold, as much as he thought they could possibly carry, as well as parched grain, dates and nuts to trade for meat and water along their journey. Gold and myrrh were no use if you were dying of hunger or thirst.

The day before their departure they had a final audience with the Queen. The swelling on her neck had mostly gone now, leaving a vivid red scar, surrounded by wrinkles of skin where the growth had stretched it. But her hair shone again. Her crown was larger and heavy with jewels, her lips were rouged, and her hands and feet were decorated in red and orange spirals, just like her aunt's. The leopard cub sat on her lap, golden-eyed and watchful.

She looked almost, thought Narmer, like the glorious queen he had first imagined.

Perhaps she saw something of that in his face, for she laughed, then clapped her hands at one of the servants standing by the smooth alabaster walls. The servant bowed and picked something up, then brought it over to her.

It was a cushion, and on it were three identical amulets on long gold chains. The servant held the cushion out to Nitho, then the Trader. Finally Narmer picked up the third amulet. It was an alabaster egg, smooth and white as the palace walls. But some skilled hand had set spiralled gold tracery, with a touch of turquoise, into the stone itself.

It was the most beautiful thing Narmer had ever seen.

He glanced at the others. Nitho was pulling hers over her head, so Narmer did as well. It felt cool against his skin.

'An amulet to take you safely home,' said the Queen lightly, as if she hadn't already given them treasure that kings would envy. 'Though I don't believe you will need it.' She smiled at them. 'I had another dream last night. A true dream, I think. You were all in it.'

'What happened in your dream, Your Majesty?' asked Nitho.

The Queen's eyes lost their focus for a moment, as though she were looking back into her dream. 'You came to Sumer safely,' she said. 'But there was more.'

She held her hand out to the Trader. The women attendants gasped — it was an unheard-of honour for the Queen to touch a man, even one who had touched her earlier to save her life. But that had been in private ...

The Trader took her hand with his usual calm.

'Good fortune, dear friend,' said the Queen quietly. 'You will have all that your heart desires. And one last journey, with a home you never expected, and joy and comfort at the end. But you will never come again to Punt.'

She took Nitho's hand now. 'You will have what you wish for most as well,' she said.

'Really?' Nitho's face was suddenly heartbreakingly eager.

'Oh, yes,' said the Queen, smiling. 'If I were you I'd hurry back to Sumer. The sooner the better, my dear. It's high time you made your offering.'

'What offering?' Narmer blurted out — then blushed. Even after all these moons with the Trader, it was still hard to remember that he was no longer a prince, no longer free to interrogate even a queen if he chose.

The Queen just smiled. 'Feed him lettuce, my dear,' she added. 'I have always found it most effective.'

She turned to Narmer but didn't offer him her hand. Narmer wasn't insulted. He was neither woman nor eunuch, and he knew the Queen had done him honour enough already. 'Your master told me that you were once a prince in your own land. You will never be a prince again, or a king either.'

Narmer reddened, and tried to ignore the pain that slashed at his heart.

'But you will be something else. They will remember your name,' said the Queen quietly, 'for more than six thousand years.'

Six thousand ... It was an impossibly large number. And the prophecy was carefully vague too. How could anyone know if their name would live that long?

'So my dreams won't come true like Nitho's and our master's?' he asked, keeping his voice respectful.

The Queen laughed. 'No, young man. They won't. You don't even know what to wish for yet. And you,' she added to Bast, who was prowling around the throne as though wondering if she should climb up onto the Queen's lap next to the leopard cub, 'you will also get something you never expected. And Queen of the Desert you may be, but you're not queen here. If you try to jump onto my throne you'll feel my foot.' She smiled. 'Take her away,' she said to Nitho. 'Goodbye, my friend,' she added to the Trader. 'If my dream is a true one we will never meet again.'

'What did the Queen mean?' Narmer whispered to Nitho, as the three of them walked through the colonnades to their rooms. 'What offering was she talking about? What did she mean about lettuce? And what is it that you and the Trader wish for?'

Nitho flushed. 'He dreams of finding his children,' she said quickly. Narmer noticed she left his other questions unanswered.

They left Punt before the dew had risen the next day.

CHAPTER 21

The Season of Flood (Summer to Autumn)

There were two ways to get to Sumer. The first was the trading route: north by sea, then through Ka'naan with its copper and turquoise mines, and down the Euphrates River by barge to the Trader's home town of Ur, bringing the metals as well as the precious building stone from upriver that the town prized.

But this time there was no need for more trading. They would cross the sea in the Queen's own ship, inlaid with gold and ebony, then head straight across the drylands to Sumer. A journey that might take a year or more around the coast would take no more than three or four moons. It would be hard going, of course. But the land was familiar to the Trader.

'The master knows every well and water seep along the route,' said Nitho. They were eating watermelon slices in the prow of the ship, while the Trader napped under a shelter of red and gold cloth. The cat was sprawled at Nitho's feet, chewing the stuffed quails left over from breakfast.

The waves lapped the boat's sides below them. The air smelt of the rose oil that the Queen's sailors sprinkled on the sails, and of cat.

Narmer spat a few seeds over the prow into the waves. 'How does the master remember everything?' He had been meaning to ask this for many moons. 'He can remember the names of every person he's traded with, and what he bought and how much he paid. It's almost magic.'

Nitho looked at him sharply, then grinned. She wore her usual travelling clothes, but had yet to pull the scarf across her face that turned her into a boy. 'Want to know the secret?'

'Of course,' said Narmer, surprised. He thought that she was about to tell him a chant that would help keep the information in his memory. But instead she reached down to the pouch at her belt. She handed him a scrap of leather, tanned and scraped thin and rolled so tightly it was no bigger than a twig.

Narmer threw his melon rind overboard, licked the stickiness off his fingers and wiped them on his tunic. He unrolled the leather carefully, making sure he didn't tear it. It had been marked with a knife, but not with a pretty design. In fact some of the marks looked like the number tallies from home that the priests used to record how many pots of grain each farmer stored in the palace silo, or like the pictures used to mark the King's name.

Narmer stared at it, understanding seeping in.

Nitho took the scrap from him. 'They're words, and a map,' she said. 'See? A map is a picture of the land. This is the sea, these are rivers, and these are towns. That is your River there, the long line; that is Thinis. This is the way we are heading: east to Sumer. These marks here stand for words. That is the mark for a mine, and those wavy lines mean a waterhole.'

Narmer stared at the tiny mark that had been his home. 'Will the master mind that you showed me?'

Nitho shook her head. 'He wants you to learn to write. But you're still learning to speak Sumerian. It's hard to learn too much at once.'

'How many different marks are there?'

Nitho shrugged. 'Lots. There are marks for everything you can trade, or grow, and for people and animals too. I'll teach you more when we get home. Or our master will.'

When we get home . . .

Narmer gazed out at the waves.

What was waiting for them in Sumer? The Trader was rich now beyond his wildest dreams. He had even lost the distracted look he had worn since leaving Thinis. And when he gazed at Narmer now it was with calm satisfaction.

What would happen to Narmer if the Trader decided not to travel any more? Would he have to find another trader to teach him? Or would their master find other work for him in Sumer? Would he become a workman, supervising slaves or planting melon crops?

There was so much he didn't know. But pride — and respect for the Trader — made it impossible to ask.

The crossing was smooth; the captain knew the weather signs and never travelled if there was a breath of storm. Then they said goodbye to the crew and travelled up through the mountains, between blighted rocks and cliffs that seemed to stare at them as they passed. Other travellers might be in danger from bandits here, but the Queen had sent guards to protect them.

From the mountains they descended to the drylands: stretches of sand in high-piled dunes enough like the country around Thinis for Narmer to feel a pang; then across dry rocklands with hills like blasted skulls. Here the Queen's men left them to travel by themselves.

From here it would be slow going for the porters, weighted down with the heavy packs of gold, as well as the tents, spears and water. The others carried the lighter packs of myrrh and food, but each night Narmer still felt his shoulders ache with the unaccustomed load.

It was late summer now — hot days and cold nights — and there were no trees to give wood to burn. They collected dry animal droppings as they walked instead, or branches of wormwood and other shrubs, but even so, most nights there wasn't enough fuel for a fire.

Sometimes there were fingers of ice in their goatskin waterbags in the morning. What must winter be like here? wondered Narmer. The bitter wind and the clear desert sky tried to suck the warmth from their bones. But at least they slept in warm cloaks of panther skin, another gift from the Queen.

Their food was a handful of dried dates at morning, noon and night, with nuts and melon seeds that had been dried and baked in mutton fat and honey: travelling food from Punt. Water was measured drop by drop, to make it last till the next oasis.

Oases meant water — thin seeps from a cliff face, or sometimes a spring or even a pool. Water meant animals, and animals meant dried dung for the tiny fires that hardly drove away the darkness. But fire meant that the travellers could have bread to eat, cakes baked quickly in hot ashes, tasting of sand and reminding Narmer of home.

Oases meant other people, too, the nomads who lived in this harsh land, hunting and driving their herds of scrawny cattle and even scrawnier goats from waterhole to waterhole, across the shattered stonelands, the dry river beds, the stone chasms of the mountains.

But the nomads respected the porters' spears and the Trader's knowledge of medicines. They longed for a touch of beauty, and the travellers traded strings of beads and alabaster pots for the privilege of joining the nomads at their waterholes, sharing their fires or their meat.

But even without the beads and the medicine the scattered dwellers of this harsh land were eager to share what little they had with a stranger, for nothing more than a story around the fire — or hoping that they too might be given hospitality when they needed it.

They're so much friendlier than the People of the Sand, thought Narmer. Or are they? he wondered suddenly. Apart from one short meeting, he had only known the People of the Sand as enemies, not as hosts around their campfires.

It was customary to give a guest the fattest portion of the meat, the warmest spot in the camel-skin tents. And in return the Trader's party left the best they had to offer: not myrrh or gold, which the nomads had not use for, but bags of parched grain, dried to make it lighter on their travels, or ointment for sore eyes, or honeycomb or goat's cheese wrapped in wax: the sorts of luxuries that the big-eyed children of the waterholes had rarely seen.

It was a hard journey, but a good one. The Trader's knowledge and their trade goods meant that they were never seriously short of water. Nid, Jod and Portho hunted too, catching ibex and deer, and once a wild camel which the travellers shared with the people at the next oasis. Even the cat brought game back sometimes, as the fancy took her.

And now Narmer mostly walked. The muscles that the crocodile had taken would never return, but he had built up other muscles to compensate. He would never be much of a runner. Yet his leg now moved when he wanted it to. It ached in the cold, but there was no more agony.

He still had not found the courage to ask the Trader what would happen to him when they reached Sumer. Part of him was afraid that the Trader might be offended. It was up to a master, after all, to look after his dependants. Another part of him just wanted to enjoy the journey. These days seemed almost beyond time, as though they would walk and hunt and laugh companionably around the night-time fire forever.

Slowly the land sloped downwards. They were nearing Sumer now. Drylands gave way to grass, blasted plateaux to hills. And finally the grass turned into marshlands: green-black mud and beds of reeds where snakes slept in the sun and birds rose in endless clouds as the Trader's party approached. The smell of rotting vegetation seeped into their clothes. The path was hard to follow sometimes. But now it *was* a path, beaten by travellers like themselves, and herders and their animals, and wild goats and sheep.

Mosquitoes sipped at their skin. All of them now wore scarves like Nitho's across their faces to try to keep off the ravenous small beasts. But even then they crept inside each crevice. The only thing that really kept them off was plastered mud, which stank, so that it was hard to know which was worse.

'There's a story that a mighty warrior stole a wife away from a neighbouring tribe,' said the Trader one day from behind his scarf. 'He hid her in the marshes, but she kept complaining that she was lonely with no companions. She whined so loudly that the gods took pity on her, and sent her ...'

'Let me guess: a cloud of mosquitoes for company,' said Narmer, grinning.

'There's an oil made from scented grass that keeps them off,' offered Nitho.

'Where is it? Why aren't we using it?' demanded Narmer.

Nitho looked surprised. 'We used up the last of it long before we got to Thinis. But we can get more once we're home.'

'Not long now.' The Trader's eyes were bright. Nid, Jod and Portho chattered excitedly to each other, pointing out familiar landmarks.

Home. They had travelled for so long now it seemed impossible that the journeying might end. And what then? thought Narmer. What is waiting for me in Sumer?

They camped that night on ground that had seemed dry the night before. But by morning the damp had seeped into the panther skins. Even their clothes were wet and stank of the marshes. The cat was already prowling around the tents, mewing her discontent. She had found some small creature to eat in the night, and her whiskers were red with drying blood.

'Should we hang the tents out to dry before we set out?' asked Narmer. Goatskin rotted if rolled up wet.

But the Trader shook his head. 'Leave them. We'll be home by afternoon.'

Narmer felt his heart beat as fast as a mob of deer running from a hunter. He had no idea what he felt. Relief, curiosity, terror ...

They ate the last of the travel food — there was no need to ration it now — and started to walk again. By mid-morning the land had begun to rise once more. The path led up a hill — tiny after the mountains they had crossed, but higher than the marshes they had just travelled through.

They reached the top and Narmer gasped.

The fields of Sumer lay before them.

CHAPTER 22

Sumerian Season of Ploughing (Autumn)

Narmer had known that Sumer was rich, that wheat and barley grew there just as they had at Thinis. But he had never expected anything like this.

Field after field, all the way to the horizon. And instead of one river there were hundreds, strangely regular streams of water, green as mint leaves, which led through rectangles of brown, ploughed ground where grain would grow, stretches of vegetables, of vines, fruit trees and melons.

Narmer shook his head. What sort of land was this, where even the rivers formed a pattern like tiles in a courtyard?

The Trader's face wore the contented smile of a man who has journeyed across the world and now is back again. 'The canals are still full,' he said. 'A good flood means a good crop.'

'Canals?' The word was unfamiliar.

The Trader laughed. 'You don't think these water courses are natural, do you? Canals are dug by man. They drain the flood water from the farms in wet times, and carry it from the river to water the crops in dry.'

'The river?'

'The Euphrates. It's still too far away to see,' said Nitho.

Narmer gazed at the fields in front of him. It was almost impossible to accept! The sheer scale of the farmland, the thought that mere humans had transformed a world like this ...

He suddenly imagined what Thinis could do with canals like these, to take water from the River into the drylands, beyond the reach of the flood. Or storing floodwaters, maybe, so that ...

He shook his head. No more thoughts of Thinis! This was his life now, whatever it was going to be.

They started down the hill. The path became a road as they travelled through the farmland, as good as the main street of Thinis.

Suddenly Narmer stared again. There on the road in front of them was a wild donkey — no, a tamed donkey — but who had ever thought of taming an animal like a donkey? The big beast was pulling something behind it. Not dragging it, but ... He squinted and tried to understand.

'Shut your mouth before the flies rush in. It's just a cart on wheels,' said Nitho. She looked like she was enjoying his amazement.

'Wheels?'

'Wheels go round and round. The carts go on top. Carts can carry more than a laden donkey.' Nitho grinned. 'You can even ride in one.'

Narmer gulped as the donkey and the cart passed them. The animal was being led by a small child. How could someone so young control a donkey?

'There are lots of tame donkeys in Sumer,' added Nitho kindly. 'They're useful for carrying things.'

'But how . . .' Narmer shut his mouth. He wasn't going to appear even more ignorant by asking further questions. But what else had this extraordinary land to show him? No, he was no prince now. In Sumer it seemed he was as ignorant as any of the People of the Sand.

They walked all day, and still there was no sign of the city. Just fields, worked by farmers dressed in loincloths and headdresses and nothing more, guiding cattle that had been tamed to pull a plough. Incredible, thought Narmer. These ploughs were so much bigger than the hand-held ploughs of Thinis, and made of metal, not wood. There were more canals, and then still more, and yet more fields, so that they seemed as though they'd continue to the far end of the world.

Dotted among the fields were houses woven from reeds, and others with mud walls like in Thinis, and thatched with reed roofs or rounded mud-brick roofs like the round ovens at home.

And at last the Euphrates River appeared in the distance. Narmer stared at it — so like his own River, and so unlike as well. It ran between boulders, which looked like pebbles at this distance, and it gleamed brown and blue and green.

More tame donkeys passed them, sometimes laden with panniers instead of pulling the strange carts. There were people in tunics like Nitho's and the Trader's, who raised their hands in salute and called out words of greeting as they went by. There were dark men like Jod and Nid and

Portho, dressed in leopard skins. Naked children from neighbouring farms ran after them, with juice-stained faces and muddy feet, shrieking with happy terror when Bast turned round to glare and hiss.

Clouds began to gather above them, dark as silt. Thunder grumbled over the hills. Narmer shivered. He was getting used to storms and rain — almost. But he still longed sometimes for the ever-blue skies of Thinis, where water came neatly down the River, instead of leaking from the sky.

And finally, there in the distance was the city of Ur.

Narmer had been looking at it for a while, he realised, but had taken it for a hill, not a town. Somehow he had been expecting a city of alabaster, like Punt. These walls were the colour of mud, like in Thinis. But how could mud walls be so massive? What kept them from crumbling down?

Suddenly the air above was torn by a glare of lightning, cleaving the sky in two. But the thunder and lightning were appropriate, Narmer thought. A city like this deserved a drum roll from the sky.

'We'll go round to the Western Gate,' said the Trader casually.

'How many gates are there?' Narmer asked before he could stop himself.

'Five main ones. But the Western Gate is closest to the Temple of Nanna.'

'Are we going to give thanks for our journey?'

The Trader smiled. 'That too. No, the priests of Nanna will store our valuables. It's the only place where they'll be safe. No one would dare steal from Nanna. The priests will keep them till we need them — after a suitable gift has been offered, of course.'

The walls grew higher and higher as the travellers drew closer, till finally the city towered above them. The road grew wider too, and was crowded with more people even than Punt — men with bunches of grapes strung on poles or strings of freshly caught carp, women with baskets of fresh figs, people walking, riding or being carried in the curious cart affairs.

The Western Gate was as wide as a courtyard, and made of wood fixed with bronze, Narmer noticed, not lashed together with cord like back in Thinis. It opened onto a market place filled with potters, whirling clay on wheels a little like the ones on the carts. Almost magically, it seemed, the twirling clay rose to become pots — tall pots, wide pots, round pots ... Other potters painted or dipped their pots in glaze, while their young apprentices carried trays of completed ware over to the kilns, or placed newly fired pots out for display.

Narmer's eyes filled with amazement. Potters in Thinis formed their pots from coils of clay, smoothed by hand. None was as fine as this. And so many! A hundred pots, a thousand pots ... more pots than there were numbers in the world to count! How many people must live in Ur, thought Narmer wonderingly, to use as many pots as these? He had thought Punt was huge. But this ...

They continued through the marketplace (Bast keeping close to Nitho now, lifting each paw with distaste and twitching her whiskers at all the noise), and along an adjoining street, where stallholders called out as they passed, offering baked chickpeas or fresh breads, sesame pastries or skewers of honeyed lamb.

The city seemed to go on forever. But to Narmer's relief the Temple soon loomed in front of them, its whitewashed mud walls more massive than he had thought any building could possibly be, and higher too, its walls rising step after step almost to the sky.

Once inside the Temple, it was all business.

Dark-robed priests with wet clay tablets glided up to them to take their heavy packs, and weigh their gold and their myrrh. Their eyes opened wide at the sheer quantity of riches the Trader had brought back. An acolyte rushed off to find the chief priest. He was the tallest man Narmer had ever seen, dressed in white linen with long stripes of red and purple. But even he seemed speechless at the sheer quantity of riches. He'd have bowed, thought Narmer, if it hadn't been beneath his dignity as a servant of the god.

'You will want to make an offering for your safe arrival,' the chief priest suggested.

The Trader nodded casually. But Narmer could see his eyes crinkle with enjoyment. 'Shall we say a score of oxen?'

The chief priest's eyes widened even further. 'Honoured sir! May your name live a thousand years!'

Another acolyte ran to bring fine mugs of fruit juice, and plates of grapes and figs. No one even commented when the cat sharpened her claws on the wall hangings.

Bags of gold were weighed out for Jod and Nid and Portho — but not, observed Narmer, for Nitho and him.

Finally, when all was counted, the chief priest handed a small clay tablet with the final tally to the Trader, and pressed the mark of his ring at the bottom to seal the bargain. The acolytes bowed them to the doors, still wide-eyed with wonder.

It was time to go home.

But will it be *my* home? wondered Narmer, as they walked back down the steps of the Temple. He was desperate for the Trader to give him some clue about what awaited him.

He glanced at the others. Jod, Nid and Portho were joking among themselves, and calling out greetings to people they knew. The Trader wore the relaxed look of one who has his old familiar world around him once more — and who has a life of prosperity to look forward to. Nitho looked far younger than she had ever seemed before, drinking in all the sights and sounds of home. She noticed him looking at her, and smiled. 'Not long now.'

Even Bast looked pleased, loping in front of them as though she were in charge of the party and their destination. She had grabbed a grilled fish from somewhere, and carried it like a trophy.

But all Narmer felt was emptiness. In every other place they'd visited, all of them had been strangers. But now the only stranger was him.

Despite the crowds, he had never felt so alone.

They went out through another city gate — different from the one they had entered by. There were more ploughed fields of rich brown dirt, and more canals. Geese paddled past old men with fishing lines. Small boys sailed toy boats. Narmer found it strange to walk without the weight of a pack on his back. Strange to smell moist ploughed soil again, yet with a slightly foreign tang.

They passed through groves of pomegranate trees, their leaves yellowing with the autumn, their fruit swelling fat and red. A cart rumbled past them, piled high with the big long melons they had enjoyed so much in Punt.

They kept on walking. The ground began to rise again. And now there were no canals. The dusty mud-brick houses were smaller and surrounded by groves of dates or carobs, trees that could survive without much water.

Finally they came to a small hill. It was crowned with an orchard of pistachio trees, their red leaves drifting to the ground. Amid the trees was a mud-walled house, small but well looked after, with smoke drifting up from a cooking fire in its courtyard, and the smell of fresh bread wafting through the air.

The cat bounded ahead. She strolled through the door of the house as though she owned it.

There was a cry. An old man peered out, followed by an old woman with no teeth. They eyed the travellers for a few seconds, then ran towards them, trying to bow and laugh at the same time.

'Master Nammu!' cried the man. 'You are back! You are safe! And Mistress Nitho! Welcome! How good it is to see you at last!'

The Trader smiled. 'I can see how well you have cared for my home, good Simo and Thammer,' he said. 'But there is someone else you must meet as well.'

The Trader put his wrinkled hand on Narmer's shoulder. 'This is Narmer. From this day forward he is my son, as

Nitho is my daughter. The children of my old age, and my heart.'

It was as though the earth had opened under Narmer's feet. He felt the Trader's thin arms embracing him, and dazedly embraced him back. It felt strange after calling him 'Master' for so long.

The Trader hugged Nitho too. She was crying, but she showed none of the shock that Narmer felt. She must have half expected this, thought Narmer. She's really been living as his daughter since she was a baby. It's just an acknowledgment of the way things have always been.

But me ...

The Trader gazed from him to Nitho and back again. His crinkled face, once so expressionless, was wet with tears. 'I've spent so many years searching. And now at last I will have a home and fortune worthy to offer a family. Welcome, my children. Welcome home.'

CHAPTER 23

Narmer's bedroom was small, its tiles worn by years of use. The paint on the mud walls had faded. But there was clean linen, and when Narmer opened the shutters he could see a gleam of moonlight on a far-off canal.

He was tired, but he couldn't sleep. He stood at the window instead, trying to remember what he'd seen out there before the sun set.

This would be his new life, then: the son of a newly rich merchant in what must be the greatest city in the world. In some ways it was better than being a prince of Thinis.

He should be rejoicing, he knew. But instead it all seemed so strange he couldn't think how to enjoy it. What would he do with himself now?

It had been many moons since he had dreamt of his homeland and woken expecting to find himself back in his bed in the palace. So why were things different now his journey had ended? Why did it seem as though Thinis had been wrenched from him a second time?

Did he want Nammu as a father? Narmer smiled in the darkness. For the most part Nammu was as unlike his own father as it was possible to be. But both men had strength — and wisdom — in their own way. And Narmer respected the Trader with a depth he knew could soon be love.

His kingdom had been torn from him, leaving wounds that bled more fiercely than the bite from the crocodile. And he had torn himself from his family . . .

And now it seemed as though the gods had given him back a family and kingdom of quite a different kind. The Trader as a father, and Nitho . . .

A sister, Narmer told himself. Sister and friend. He smiled in the darkness. He hadn't even admitted to himself, he realised, how much he would have missed Nitho if he'd had to go and work for someone else. Nitho, with her brown hands and laughing eyes.

Yes, he decided, he *was* happy here. Or would be, when he got used to the idea.

And if he still felt as though his heart were bleeding . . . well, he had already coped with one great change in his life. And after all, this one was a change for the better.

But in many ways being the son of a rich merchant was surprisingly *similar* to being a prince of Thinis.

He had thought the Trader — or Father Nammu, as he now called him — would buy a richer farm among the canals with all his newfound wealth. But when he suggested this Nammu just smiled.

'This house was my father's, and my grandfather's. I like it here.'

'But we could have our own fish ponds!' objected Narmer. Even in Sumer, with its bustling markets, you needed your own land, your beehives, fish ponds and women weaving flax, to produce what you needed to live well.

Nammu's smile grew wider. 'Exactly. So the canals can come to us.'

This was Narmer's job, then: to find engineers to design two great canals, running from the nearest existing canals to Nammu's dry land. Then he hired workmen to construct them.

It was a massive job, but there was gold enough to pay for whatever was needed. And one thing Narmer had learnt back in Thinis was how to supervise teams of men.

Why did I ever think I might be without anything to do? thought Narmer, as he checked the workmen's progress one morning. Already the first canal was almost finished. Soon the men would dig out the final cubits that separated it from the existing canal network, and fresh cool water would flow onto their barren lands. 'Tomorrow, then?' he asked the foreman.

The man nodded. 'One more day will do it. Won't be much of a flow at this time of year. But when the floods come in spring you can trap the water in the dykes. That'll give you all you need.'

Narmer smiled. Already the new orchard boundaries had been marked out with white stones, and the fish ponds had been dug. He could just imagine what canals like this would have meant to Thinis. So much more land could have been planted with grain, with fruit trees ...

He shut his mind to the thought.

The Trader was already breakfasting in the courtyard when Narmer arrived back at the house — a grander house by far these days, its mud walls painted blue and red, with new rooms and fresh tiles on the floors, rich wall hangings and carpets, and this courtyard with its flowers and fountains.

Nammu looked up from his bread and goat's cheese and sliced onions, and smiled. He dyed his beard purple now, to indicate the family's wealth, and sweetened his breath with shreds of cinnamon bark. But he still had the wrinkled brown skin of a man who had spent his life crossing the deserts.

'How is the work, my son?'

Narmer grinned. He sat down on one of the couches and sliced a stuffed cucumber onto some fig bread. 'One more day and the first canal will be finished. We'll have to celebrate.' He looked around him. 'Where's Nitho?'

After their long journey together Nitho had had no intention of keeping to the women's quarters. Bast was sprawled on the tiles, hunched over a bowl of goose guts. But there was no sign of her mistress.

'She's at the Temple of Inanna.' Nammu chewed his cheese and onions loudly. His voice had taken on its old inscrutability. But he seemed ... watchful. Troubled almost, thought Narmer.

'What's she doing there?'

'Making her offering.'

Narmer had almost forgotten the Queen's advice to Nitho to hurry back to Ur and make her offering. If he'd thought about it at all he'd assumed that Nitho had already done so, just as she made the offerings for the household on the altar in the courtyard every morning.

Narmer smiled as one of the servants held out a platter, and he broke off some sesame cake. He looked up to find Nammu still watching him.

'Everything is all right, isn't it?' he asked uncertainly. 'About her making her offering?' He had seen women waiting at the Temple of Inanna in Ur, just as he had in Punt: a line of them sitting on the steps ... with empty hands.

'What do the women offer to Inanna?' he asked suddenly.

Nammu hesitated. 'Themselves,' he said at last, still watching Narmer. 'Every girl must offer herself to Inanna once before she marries.'

'But ... but *how* do they offer themselves?' Narmer was confused. Most offerings to the gods were burnt on the altar. If every maiden in Sumeria were burnt before marriage there would be no Sumerians.

Again Nammu paused. Then he said reluctantly, 'She waits outside the temple until a man chooses to lie with her.' He took a small sip of his grape juice.

'Lie with her?' Suddenly Narmer understood what he meant. 'But that ... that's terrible! Horrible! To lie with a stranger ...!'

'What is an offering worth if it comes easily?' Nammu regarded him steadily now. 'But it will be even harder for a girl like Nitho. She is a good girl, with her own beauty. But few men will look beyond the scar on her face. She may have to sit in front of the Temple for many moons before someone takes pity on her, and chooses her instead of someone prettier ...'

'You mean she has to stay there until … No!' Narmer surged to his feet as though he'd seen a hippo in their fields. 'I won't let her!'

He saw Nammu's soft smile as he rushed from the courtyard.

He hadn't realised how much better his leg was until he had to run. It was painful, but at least he could do it now.

He tore out of the house and up the road, through the Eastern Gate and the Cloth Market, along the Street of Dyers, past the rope makers' stalls and the bead makers, grinding the little spheres of bone smooth before they painted them, through the Tinsmiths' Square …

His leg was screaming at him by the time he reached the corner near the Temple of Inanna. This temple was nowhere near as massive as the Temple of Nanna. But it was almost as richly decorated, long rather than tall, its mud walls painted yellow so they glowed like the moon, and decorated with a frieze depicting scenes of the Goddess's bounty — sheaves of wheat, baskets of barley, mounds of pomegranates, dates and figs.

The girls making their offering sat on the ground along the front wall, each on her mat of plaited reeds, with her basket of food and water, in case the wait was long. Most looked nervous. A few looked flirtatious, licking their lips to make them shine and patting their hair, so they would look as pretty as possible. And a couple, older than the rest, looked desperate, thought Narmer indignantly, with hopeless eyes, as though they had waited for years and still not been chosen.

A steady procession of men walked past them, gazing, laughing, nudging each other as they pointed out this girl or that. Most were tradesmen, or farmers, with simple tunics and rough beards, straggly if they were young, thick or grey if they were older, all hoping, thought Narmer furiously, to find a girl of good family — the sort they could never have hoped to approach, except at the Goddess's temple. Here and there a knot of wealthy men in linen tunics and good sandals had joined the crowd. Most of them, Narmer realised, were just there for the show, with no intention of choosing a girl. But others looked at the girls slowly and deliberately, as though enjoying this moment of power as each girl hoped to be their choice, or to be passed over till a man with kinder features came along. It was as though these men were choosing sheep, Narmer thought bitterly.

As he watched, one man with the mud-flecked arms of a potter touched a girl on the shoulder. She stood obediently, though her knuckles were white with terror as she picked up the reed mat she had been sitting on and followed him up the stairs into the Temple.

Narmer gazed along the line of girls. Yes, there was Nitho, in her best linen dress with its purple hem, and a jewelled belt, with more jewels in her ears and around her toes and ankles. She had rouged her heels and brushed her hair so it hung like a smooth curtain across her face, half hiding the scar.

But Nammu was right, thought Narmer. None of these idle men inspecting the girls would see Nitho's true beauty. One by one they'd pass her by — fat old farmers, ox tamers, basket weavers ... How dare they leer down at a girl like Nitho — and then reject her!

He tried to keep the anger from his face as he crossed the street and joined the line in front of the waiting girls. They smiled up at him, hopeful that this handsome young man might be the one to choose them.

Nitho was looking at the ground. How many times had she been hurt already today, Narmer wondered indignantly, by some stupid peasant sneering with distaste at the twist in her smile? How many men had she looked up at hopefully, only to have them walk away?

'Nitho?'

Nitho glanced up abruptly. She flushed. 'What are you doing here?' she hissed, eyes darting from side to side. 'You don't know anything about this. Go away!'

'I know enough.' Narmer tried to control his temper. 'You have to wait here till some man chooses you, right?'

Nitho nodded uncomfortably.

Narmer held out his hand. 'I am a man. And I choose you.'

Something unfathomable flared in Nitho's eyes. Her face flushed an even deeper red. She put her hand in his, then struggled to her feet. For once, thought Narmer, she looked as if words had failed her.

'Do we have to go in there?' Narmer looked in disgust as another couple ascended the steps to the Temple.

'No. No, that's only when there is nowhere else to go.'

'Then we'll go home,' said Narmer firmly, leaning down to pick up her mat and basket. It was a struggle to keep his voice steady. The Sumerians were his people now, he reminded himself. It would cause harm to the family to show disgust.

But it was difficult.

They crossed the road, still hand in hand. Narmer could hear the envious chatter of the girls behind them. The ugly one had been taken — and by such a beautiful young man, with gold at his neck and an alabaster amulet on his chest!

He shot a quick glance at Nitho. Her face looked different. Almost joyous, he thought wonderingly, but scared too. Relieved, he assumed, to be away from there.

They were through the Markets and out the Gate before Narmer let her hand fall. 'Done,' he said, breathing more easily. 'Now no one will ever know.'

'Know what?'

He looked at her in surprise. 'That we fooled them, of course. You're officially a woman now, without having to go through that horrible ritual.'

'You mean you don't . . .' Nitho's voice broke off.

'I don't want . . .' what was the phrase? 'to lie with you?' Narmer took her hand again. 'Nitho, how could you think I'd do such a thing? I just wanted to save you. You don't really think you need to sacrifice yourself . . .'

'You . . . you idiot!' yelled Nitho.

She wrenched her hand away, lifted her skirts and ran down the road to home, leaving him staring after her, the mat and basket still in his hand.

CHAPTER 24

Things were different after that.

Nammu seemed happy, watching his newly watered fields flourish, seeing his adopted son command the men in his fields. Nitho too went about her daily business, overseeing the women at their weaving and cooking and washing. She arranged to have the house repainted a pale blue, with fresh tiles for the courtyard where they ate together, adorned with patterns of leaping cats and date palms.

She was as friendly as before, after a few days of stiffness and embarrassment. But somehow the easy comradeship of the journey had gone.

Had she really thought that he would lie with her?

From time to time Narmer caught himself looking at her, wondering. He had never thought of her like that — or, if he had, had stopped himself at once. Surely Nammu had other plans for his son and daughter.

Narmer supposed the day would come when Nammu would choose partners for them both: a son and daughter of another trading house, perhaps, with wealth that might almost match their own. Narmer's limp was hardly noticeable now, and Nitho's dowry would be so large that any family would overlook her scars.

Perhaps there might even be a husband who would value her command of languages too, allow her to organise trading trips as well as supervise her women as they ground the wheat and barley ... He would have to be special, thought Narmer, to be worthy of Nitho.

So far Nammu had made no mention of marriages. Perhaps he enjoyed having a son and daughter in his house too much to think of letting Nitho go off to a husband's home now.

But since the day at the Temple the calm pattern of their life had changed, as a pebble thrown into a pond might break up a still reflection.

The seasons turned. The second canal was finished in time for the spring floods. Then Narmer hired a foreman to supervise the autumn ploughing. Ebu was an able man, and able to teach his young master Sumerian skills like cattle breeding and beehive craft, and the art of reinforcing dyke walls with the reed mats that allowed the mud walls of Sumer to be so much higher than those at Thinis.

Before he knew it, Narmer had been in Ur more than a year. Sometimes it seemed as if his younger self had arrived only yesterday, gazing like a yokel at the wonders of the city. But at other times it was as though he had always lived here, planning expeditions with his adopted father, managing their estate.

Narmer studied at the Temple of Nanna too, like many wealthy young Sumerians, learning the history of the land: the story of the flood that cleansed the world, how the Sumerians had travelled from their original land far away to conquer the people of Akkadia and found the cities of Ur, Uruk, Eridu and Kish.

Nammu also taught Narmer merchant craft, in long conversations over honey beer and sesame bread in their flowered courtyard. Narmer learnt to write trading symbols, and to draw maps of the lands around — the cities of the Elamites, the remaining Akkadian towns, the realm of the Salouir folk to the south, Ka'naan to the northwest as well as Punt to the south. He could even add Thinis and the towns along the River to his map now, without feeling a pang of loss.

He was taught how to trade with city merchants, too: a measure of barley for a pot, or so many silver shekels for an ingot of tin. Other merchants borrowed from Nammu, giving him a third of the profits from their travels in return for the shekels to buy their trade goods. And Narmer watched and learnt.

Nitho was always part of these trade negotiations, sitting on her chair with the men, translating when necessary, and offering her opinions on what would fetch the best price where.

It was a good life, with companionship and satisfying work. And if Narmer ever heard a whisper in his mind of homesickness, a longing to share his new skills with his own land, he had trained himself to ignore it.

* * *

Marduk the trader was an old friend of Nammu's, a giant man with a salt and pepper beard and a laugh that shook the house. Once he and Nammu had been competitors. But tonight Marduk seemed happy at his friend's success.

Marduk had just returned from his latest trip and the two men had spent the day exchanging stories — tales of women warriors north of the Great Blue, with hair the colour of the moon, or cloth as fine as mist made by caterpillars in a land some said was far beyond the rising sun.

Now the afternoon's feast was crumbs and bones. The sleepy servants had lit the oil lamps and put out trays of dates stuffed with almonds, the season's first raisins, goat's cheeses pressed with poppyseeds, and radishes with sesame. The cat lay on her back under the table, her legs in the air and her whiskers stained with mutton fat and quail.

Nitho had excused herself and gone to bed. Narmer was getting up to leave too when some words of Marduk's caught his attention. 'And did you hear about young Kuumas?' Marduk asked, pouring himself another mug of beer.

Nammu shook his head.

'Thought he'd try to follow in your footsteps. Took an expedition across the desert to that river.' The big man chuckled. 'That's what they call it, don't they? Just "The River". As though there were no other rivers in the world.'

Nammu glanced at Narmer. 'Not much to trade for there. Only gold, and there are closer mines than that.'

'That's what we all said. But he wouldn't be told. Nearly lost everything, including his life. Said the River towns were warring among themselves. No one had any time for spices and precious goods, and no gold to pay for them anyway.'

Narmer was surprised to see his hand was trembling. He put his mug down carefully on the low table. 'Did he tell you the names of the warring towns?'

Marduk noticed the urgency in his voice. 'That's right, you're from down that way, aren't you? No, he didn't mention names. Knew they'd mean nothing to me anyway. Don't know where Kuumas is now either. He was in Punt when I last saw him ...'

An hour later Nammu saw his friend to the guest rooms. He returned to the courtyard to find Narmer still sitting there, staring absently at the moon's reflection in the canal. Nammu seated himself beside his adopted son and watched him for a few moments. 'There are many towns along the River, my son,' he said at last. 'The fighting might have been a long way from Thinis.'

Narmer didn't look at him. 'I know. But Father Nammu, Thinis is the biggest of all the towns on the River. A trader would go there, if anywhere.'

'Big enough to defeat an attacker, then. And Kuumas is a fool. He'd try to sell myrrh to an ant hill and ignore the palace over the hill. He may never even have got to Thinis.'

Narmer did look at Nammu then. 'I know, Father. The River is a long way away. And our lives are here.' He stood up, then bent over and embraced the old trader. 'Goodnight, Father.' He hesitated, then added, 'Thank you. For everything.'

Maybe it was the rich food, or Marduk's strange tales of faraway lands ... but Narmer couldn't get the news about the River out of his head.

Suddenly he dreamt.

He was back in the wadi where he had first met Nitho, climbing up the hills again to gaze down upon Thinis.

But it wasn't there.

There was marshland where fields should have been. Beds of reeds instead of a palace. And lurking in the reeds was the crocodile. But this time it had the face of his brother.

Grief washed through him like floodwater down the River. And with grief came wakefulness. He woke, sweating, and gulped water from the beaker next to his bed. He lay down again and tried to sleep.

It was just a dream, no more. How silly to let a dream upset him. Of course the fighting was nowhere near Thinis. Of course the town was still there, still prosperous — his father on his throne, old Seknut bossing the palace women, the smells from the bakers' ovens ...

Life had changed for him, but not for the town of his birth. And yet ...

It was no use. He swung his legs off the bed and walked out to the terrace. He could see the moon from here, the great god Nanna. The god's light poured a rain of silver onto the fields of Sumer.

A place of peace. An alliance of four cities, his adopted father had explained, strong because they worked together.

Nammu's lands, which would be Narmer's some day, rich and fertile. His future.

Narmer shook his head. Who was he trying to fool?

Until tonight he had convinced himself he had been simply glad to have a place in the world again: to be heir to fine estates, part of a new family, with the challenge and the pleasure of learning the trader's craft and caring for his adoptive father's wealth.

Now, suddenly, he knew deep down he was still Prince Narmer of Thinis. He had spent most of his life learning to think of the land's Ma'at instead of himself. Every cart he saw carrying a load, every ox he noticed ploughing a field he secretly longed to take back to the land of his birth, to show his people how valuable such things might be. Mirrors, bronze spearheads, metal ploughs, even the method of building in steps using reed mats as reinforcing, and the intricate canals to take water to lands that would otherwise be too dry to grow things — all were gifts he wanted to give to the land that bore him.

He wanted to go home.

Not forever, he told himself, as he turned from the terrace to go back to bed. Just long enough to see whether Kuumas's news about the fighting along the River was true; to assure his father that his son was well and happy; to give Seknut a gift — alabaster beads perhaps. And, if he were honest, to show Hawk that his brother had triumphed in a world far bigger than Thinis.

But he would come back to Ur in the end. His future was here, in this land of wonders between the great rivers of Tigris and Euphrates.

He would go to Thinis as a trader, not as its prince. But he would take what he knew that Thinis needed, not what would bring the most gold. And this last journey would surely convince him that Thinis was his no more. That his place was here, his people were here, his future ...

One more adventure, he thought, as he closed his eyes, eager once more for sleep. I am still too young, after all, to settle down. I'll ask Nammu for a year's leave of absence. Then I will return here for good.

'To Thinis?'

'Please, Father.'

Nammu's eyes usually crinkled with happiness when he heard the word 'Father'. But not this time.

Narmer tried to find the words to persuade him. 'For most of my life they were my people. Let me make sure Thinis is safe, and give them this one gift of knowledge, then I'll come home.'

Nammu closed his eyes. When he opened them again the brief flash of pain was gone. It was almost, thought Narmer wonderingly, as though Nammu had expected this moment, had been saving up the memories of the past year to console him while his son was gone.

And perhaps he had known, thought Narmer suddenly, remembering the Queen's words back in Punt about her 'true dream'. She had been right when she predicted that Nammu would find his children; was it also true that Narmer's name would be known for six thousand years? Had the Trader expected that Narmer would want more than a peaceful life overseeing a rich farm?

For suddenly it was as though Nammu had been planning just this trip for his son. He didn't even — as Narmer had half expected — offer to go too.

'Very well. But you should go via Ka'naan,' he said abruptly, his voice carefully expressionless. 'I know this isn't a trading journey, but trade as you go nonetheless. Remember, a trader is safer than an ordinary traveller. I'll send messengers upriver to all my acquaintances, telling them to expect you and asking them to give you what help they can.'

Narmer embraced him joyfully. Nammu felt smaller these days, as though he had shrunk while Narmer had grown.

'Thank you, Father,' was all Narmer said. But that said it all.

He told Nitho his plans too. But though her eyes widened for an instant, she simply nodded, and made a comment about the most profitable mines to visit on the way.

It took five moons to get the trade goods assembled, the messages sent out. Spring once more filled the air with scents of greenery and warm air. The hills were still dappled with the bright hues of winter wildflowers, reds and yellows and the occasional flash of blue. The fields were rich with winter crops.

Impatience nibbled at him, but he tried to control it. He had learnt enough now to know that there was no hurrying the preparations for a journey as long as this.

To his relief, Nid, Jod and Portho all volunteered to come as well. They had no need to make another journey; their families were more comfortable than they had ever expected after the last journey with the Trader. Narmer was touched by their loyalty and glad of their company. He had learnt a lot from his adopted father, but the porters' experience would be invaluable.

This time he would take tame donkeys, both for riding and to carry the trade goods — no myrrh or ebony this time, but bronze spearheads, mirrors, metal shovels and ploughs. There was no need to pack the other gifts — the skills of building canals, wheels, carts and tall buildings, and of writing, to ensure that these skills and the deeds of men could be passed on.

Finally the day came to leave. Ten donkeys were loaded with their packs and the three porters stood by them ready to depart.

Narmer gave his new father a final hug.

'I will be back, Father,' he assured him.

There were tears in the old trader's eyes. But he looked strangely calm, as though he had been preparing for this day for a long time.

'Till we meet again, my son,' he replied.

They embraced, then Narmer strode over towards the donkeys. And stopped.

There was one more animal than he had expected, with a small figure sitting on its back.

Nitho.

She was dressed in her boy's robes, and Bast was prowling around the donkeys, as though to say, *You are tethered, but I am free.*

'I'm coming too,' said Nitho stiffly. 'You'll need a translator. And ...' she flushed, '... and anyway, I'm coming too.'

'*Mmmrr?*' said the cat. She brushed against Narmer's legs, then, impatient to leave, began to slink down the road in her familiar 'following ahead' prance.

Narmer glanced back at Nammu. But his adopted father showed no surprise at the sight of Nitho on her donkey. It seemed as if he had been preparing for this as well.

'Thank you,' said Narmer. It didn't seem enough. But he wasn't sure what he felt ... and he was quite sure he had no words for whatever it might be.

Then they left.

CHAPTER 25

It was a good journey.

It was far easier travelling on a donkey, Narmer found, than being carried in a chair. His old injuries didn't bother him at all these days, except after an extra-cold night on hard ground.

They followed the River Euphrates at first, watching the barges on the water and the flocks of waterbirds across the grasslands. The river was still low, the snows that would bring the floods not yet melted. They traded beads and other trinkets in the villages for bags of barley meal, dates or skins filled with the weak barley beer of the region. But they always camped outside the walls, to give Nitho privacy from prying eyes. And besides, Bast was likely to worry the village women, who might think she planned to eat their babies as she rubbed against their legs, instead of hoping for leftovers from their stew pots.

The villages were fewer as they headed towards the headwaters of the river. This was still mostly a region of herders, driving their flocks of goats and sheep across the grasslands and sleeping in their goatskin tents. They lived on the milk and cheese from their flocks, and on wild dates and honey and the animals they hunted, and camped for part of the year to gather wild grain, spreading it out to become parched in the sun, before stuffing it into their goatskin sacks for the long summer and winter in the hills.

The travellers stayed in Ka'naan with the manager of a tin mine, one of the Trader's old friends. The way was rougher now: across plains of shattered rock, through dry wadies, seeing few people — and those they did see mostly kept clear of strangers. It must be hard living in a land that depended on rain, thought Narmer, instead of the regular floods that fed and watered the lands of Sumer and the River.

Finally they hired a ship again, to cross the sea. And then they made their slow way through the desert, towards Thinis.

Day after day there was nothing but the steady plod of the donkeys, the smell of their droppings, and of heat and rock, the sounds of wind and birds, and the sight of gazelles, which lifted their heads as the party approached and fled before the strange sight of humans who sat on animals.

Narmer learnt more about Nitho in those long days of walking than he ever had before. Somehow it was easy to talk again, with the desert around them, in the privacy of the language of the River towns, which the others didn't share. At times it was as though they were the only two people in the world.

He learnt of Nitho's early years travelling from town to town, her first memories of the Trader.

'He hugged me at night when the pain got too bad. And when people stared at my scars he told me they were signs of bravery and endurance that other people lacked. He was kinder than any father ...'

Or a father who abandoned you, thought Narmer — but didn't say it aloud. He and Nitho were regaining their old closeness now, and he didn't want to say anything that might threaten their friendship again.

In return he told her of his own childhood: running as a toddler with the women as they collected straw from the fields for the palace fires or stripped the green from the flax for the linen fibres they wove on their looms in their courtyard; watching the flint knappers as they split the stone for knives and tools and arrows, the potters as they piled up their coils of clay, turning them almost magically into pots just as the great god Khnum had breathed life into the soil of the River to create man ... all the day-to-day rhythms of life along the River.

And as their donkeys plodded close together he even tried to tell her of the feelings welling up in him, now that he was headed towards his native land ... exhilaration, fear, happiness. There were no words really to describe what he felt. But Nitho seemed to understand.

Whenever he saw a flock of herons swoop across the water now, or laughed as Bast chose the softest of their packs to sleep on, there was extra joy knowing he could share the sight with Nitho.

Perhaps it was talking of his memories that did it, but the dreams of Thinis came more often now. Sometimes he dreamed he was with his father as the King pronounced judgment on two farmers who claimed the same part of a field, or told Narmer stories about fighting off the People of the Sand. But always in those dreams the crocodile was leering from the shadows, with a face like his brother's.

Why did they always end this way? What if they were 'true dreams' like the Queen of Punt's?

He woke from these dreams sweating, staring around him in terror but seeing nothing but the sleeping forms of Nitho and the porters, or the yellow eyes of the cat as she crunched bones by the embers of the fire; and the gentle breathing of the others was enough to send him back to sleep.

CHAPTER 26

The Season of Emergence (Autumn)

The shapes of the hills were familiar. Those two, like the backside of a hippopotamus, or that one like an old man's nose ...

Narmer recognised the smells too. The breeze carried the scent of the River in flood. The light was River light again, subtly coloured by the shifting water. Even the bird calls suddenly spoke to something deep within him.

He felt as though his blood were bubbling like the overflowing River. With excitement. Nervousness. And something more. Almost without realising it he hurried ahead.

The floods would be receding now, leaving the rich black silt. The men would be checking to see if the seed was ready for planting.

Home. His home in a way that Sumer never could be. As though his heart were made of silt from the River, and its water were his blood.

He shook his head. Nonsense. Sumer *would* be his home. But this ... this was the land that had created him.

'What is it?' Nitho had caught up to him.

He shrugged. 'Remembering. That's all.' He tried to grin at her. 'Do you know where we are now?'

Nitho looked around, then flushed. 'Yes.'

'The wadi of the Oracle.' It felt like a lifetime ago. 'What would the Oracle advise me now, then?'

Nitho looked startled. Then she smiled. 'O great trader,' she intoned, 'who has conquered the vast spaces of the desert, the Oracle advises you to change into a clean tunic, and comb your beard.'

Narmer flushed, then laughed. His beard had begun growing the past year, but it still looked more like a goat's than a man's.

'You're right,' he said. He looked back at the others, and waved a hand for them to stop.

He wanted his father to see him as a wealthy man, heir to more riches than all of Thinis. He imagined his father's face as he gazed at the treasures Narmer had brought spread out before him — the metal implements, the spear heads — and as Narmer explained how Thinis too could build canals, and great walls to keep their enemies away.

Hawk might have stolen the kingdom. But Narmer would make him feel like a lizard that knew no more than its rocks.

He dressed carefully: a fine linen tunic in the Sumerian fashion that he had kept clean in his luggage, the Queen's amulet, gold rings and bracelets, sandals of plaited deer hide with red and gold tassels. He brushed as much of the dust of the desert as he could from his hair.

'Are you ready?'

It was Nitho. Narmer looked at her in astonishment. She wore women's clothes again — the pleated tunic with its purple hem that he knew was her best. She too wore her amulet from Punt, below a twist of lapis lazuli beads. There was a golden buckle on her belt and jewels in her ears and on her toes and fingers. Even her sandals looked priceless and delicate.

The clothes were familiar — he had seen her wear them when they received honoured guests, back in Sumer. He had seen them at the Temple of Inanna too. But for some reason it was as though he had never really looked at Nitho before.

He had only seen the scar at first, the crippled foot.

And when he was used to those he had also grown used to the idea of Nitho as a boyish companion, then as his sister.

Now for the first time he realised just how beautiful she was. Even the scar was beautiful, as much a part of her as the calluses from travelling or the dimples from her laughter.

'Why are you staring?' asked Nitho self-consciously. 'I thought it would be easier if I stayed in the women's quarters this time. Otherwise I'd have to share the guest quarters with you and the others. And they're too small for privacy.'

'I ...' Narmer stopped. How could he say what he felt? Did he even know what he felt?

Only that he was glad Nitho would be coming home with him as herself, not in disguise.

The donkeys were restless, stopping where there was neither shade nor water. Narmer nodded for the porters to get them moving again. He cast a last look at Nitho on her donkey, her skirts folded carefully on either side of her legs so they didn't wrinkle, and smiled.

There was all the time in the world to talk to Nitho. But now Thinis was just across the hill.

The donkeys' feet clattered against the rocky soil. Lizards stared at them from crevices, then darted to shelter.

Narmer felt his heart thump as they climbed the last hill. Up, up, till suddenly they were there, on top of the ridge.

The desert stretched behind them. In front of them the water shone like a polished bronze mirror.

But the town of Thinis had gone.

CHAPTER 27

It was just like Narmer's dream. Nothing but lumps of mud among the silt showed where the town's walls had been. A few dilapidated houses remained, but the reed thatch on top had vanished, leaving only scorch marks in their place.

No fresh green crops in the newly mud-rich fields. A few fruit trees still showed leaves, but most were skeletons, their branches bare and brown, their roots rotting. The floodwaters had taken over the defenceless town then retreated, as though they had lost interest in a land of mud and ruins.

No women pounding their washing on the banks, or gathering reeds or lotus roots. No men fishing, or naked boys aiming the shot from their slings at the water birds.

No one ...

'What happened?' asked Nitho quietly, staring at the devastation below. She had come up behind him without his noticing. The rest of the caravan with the donkeys was still toiling up the slope.

Narmer didn't reply. He wasn't sure he could speak.

'The People of the Sand?' persisted Nitho. Then she answered her own question. 'No, they don't destroy like this, burning everything in sight then leaving the River to finish the job. They don't take a whole town as slaves, or kill them. They leave the people there to sow and gather crops that they can steal some other year.'

'I'm going down,' said Narmer abruptly.

'I'll come with you ...'

'No.' For a moment he was Prince Narmer again, giving commands. 'Stay here with the others. If I'm not back by midday send Jod and Portho after me.'

'But ...' For a moment he thought she was going to argue. But then she simply nodded.

Narmer limped down the hill, alone.

His nostrils filled with the smell of fire, of flood debris that hadn't been cleaned up. This is what defeat smells like, thought Narmer. Emptiness.

Corpses would have been easier, even skeletons. At least then he'd have known what had happened to his people.

He inched quietly up the main street, his spears in his hand. Empty windows stared at him, the crumbled homes of Sithentoe the potter, Nabat the carpenter, Fenotup the baker ... all gone.

Narmer had reached the palace now. He gazed around, the tears blurring his vision.

The flood damage was less here and the signs of fire greater. These walls had been demolished by people, not water.

He dodged around a half-collapsed wall and into the First Courtyard. The long pool was mud and sand. Sand covered the tiles too. How many times had he sat with his father here? It was almost as though the King had left behind his shadow, to mingle with the ruins.

He stepped over more layers of rubble and looked around.

The guesthouse had vanished; the recent flood had taken the last vestige of the walls. The kitchen courtyard where he'd played as a child, and Seknut had fed him titbits from the pots and roasts, his own quarters, the servants' wing ... all crumbling, devastated by fire and flood. Already drifts of sand had gathered at the edges.

A child's woven reed ball sagged in a corner. It too was half filled with sand. Was it his? A keepsake, kept by Seknut in her chest?

Ghosts whispered through the shattered palace. Seknut, grumbling when he'd broken his new sandal. His father, giving judgment over which son would inherit a farmer's field. Were they real, or just the wind? It didn't matter. Their voices lingered just the same.

He wiped his eyes and looked around again, desperate to find something — anything — untouched by flames and flood. And then he saw it: a recently repaired roof, with new reeds among the old thatch, over his father's rooms.

Hope set his heart beating. Perhaps his father still lived!

He began to make his way through the ruins again, moving faster now. A snake slithered across his path then froze for a moment, surprised at a human in what was now its territory. And then it wriggled on and was lost in the rubble.

Suddenly Narmer could smell something else too. Smoke. Not old smoke from the charred wreckage, but a small fresh fire of burning dung.

Someone was cooking.

Narmer crept up to the entrance of the Royal Courtyard and peered in.

The pool here contained water, but it was scummed and green. The carob and sycamore trees still had their leaves. The bougainvillea vines were gone, the painted tiles cracked and broken.

There was a fire, small as he had suspected. And a man, crouching down and holding a stick with small birds spitted on it, their fat dripping into the flames.

His brother. All the old feelings flooded back: the pain of the crocodile attack, the sense of useless fury at what Hawk had done to him.

He stepped out of the shadows. 'Good day.'

Hawk jumped as though Narmer had cast a spear, not words. He gasped. 'You!'

'Me,' said Narmer.

'You can walk!' Hawk stared stupidly, his eyes darting from his brother's face to his rich clothes and his jewellery. Narmer wanted to bask in his brother's envy. But the ruins of Thinis had drained him of any joy. Hawk's own face was thin and shadowed. His kilt was tattered. His feet were bare and dusty.

'I can walk,' said Narmer hotly. 'I can talk too. And my hands can still throttle you.' He was inches from his brother now. 'And they will, unless you tell me ...'

'What?'

'What have you done with my people?!'

* * *

'It wasn't my fault.'

'Really?' They sat opposite each other about the fire. Hawk had offered him a share of the birds. But Narmer had refused. He wanted nothing of his brother's. Except, perhaps, the kingdom that they had now both lost.

'It was Father's fault!'

'Really?'

'Yes! The flood after you left was too high. Part of the walls collapsed. And Yebu attacked before we could fix them.'

'How did they know the walls were down?'

'Berenib.'

'Your wife!'

Hawk glanced up at him resentfully. 'Father should never have arranged the marriage. She was loyal to Yebu. Not to me.'

Or perhaps she had no reason to be loyal to you, thought Narmer.

A moment ago he had wanted to strangle his brother. Hurt him. Humiliate him. But now he saw there was no point. Hawk was a king of mud and shadows. If it was vengeance he wanted, he'd got it already.

'And Father ... ?'

Narmer knew the answer before his brother spoke. He had known it as soon as he saw the broken town. His father would have been striding through the ruins, working to rebuild. Not skulking in a sandy courtyard.

'He was killed during the attack.'

'Seknut?'

Hawk shrugged. 'I don't know. Those who weren't killed were marched off as slaves. Perhaps she was among them.'

'But you escaped.'

Hawk said nothing.

'Where is Father's grave?' For the first time Narmer let fury tinge his voice. 'Surely you gave him that much! A grave of his own!'

'The last flood took it. The flood has taken everything.'

Why do I feel grief? thought Narmer. They were lost to me anyway. Father, Thinis ... But it wasn't grief, he realised. Grief would come later. Right now there was only certainty, a strength he hadn't felt since he faced the crocodile.

He was Narmer of Thinis again. The cloak of responsibility had settled on his shoulders once more.

'Did any others escape?'

Hawk shrugged again. 'A few.' Hawk had never learnt to count more than his fingers, Narmer remembered. 'They're camped up in the hills, living wild ... Rintup and his family, Batenoe ... They bring me food sometimes.' He nodded at the skewered birds. 'For their king ...' For the first time there was real emotion in his voice: part despair, part defiance.

Narmer glanced at the green scummed pool, the crumbled walls. A king of dust and snakes, that was all his brother was now.

'Why haven't you rebuilt, then?'

'And have Yebu attack again? Or the People of the Sand? We're safer hiding.'

For the first time he met Narmer's eyes. 'Well, little brother? Are you going to tell me now that you could have saved the town? That this would never have happened if you had been king? Because it would have! It was the River that destroyed us! Not me!'

Narmer said nothing. What *would* have happened if he had been there? Would it have made a difference? Would he and his father together have seen that the dykes needed to be stronger? Could he have convinced Berenib to value her new home more than her old one?

He would never know.

And now he had come home to nothing. Death.

But he had once seen someone fight against death, he remembered. The Queen of Punt, gasping for breath on her throne.

Suddenly he knew what he should do.

Hawk glanced at Narmer's tunic, with its border of purple, the Queen's amulet on his chest. 'So, you are still a trader?'

'Yes. And now the son of the richest house of the biggest nation in the world. And that is something you can never steal from me.' He stared at his brother for a moment, and Hawk gazed back at him, eyes wide. Then he added, 'Call the others.'

'What?' Hawk still seemed lost in this new vision of his brother.

'I said call the others! Bring them here!'

'How can I call them? I don't know where they are. Up in the hills somewhere . . . ? And why do you want them?'

'Because, o King,' said Narmer calmly, 'I mean to bring our people home.'

CHAPTER 28

Narmer, Nitho and the porters set up camp by the palace's old silo, which at least still had a roof, leaving the palace ruins to Hawk. Portho and Jod built a fire from driftwood and dried roof reeds, a massive one to signal to the survivors. Nid had speared a gazelle, and set it up to roast on a makeshift spit. Bast prowled through the ruins, leaving her droppings in every sand drift, as though to tell other wildcats that this place was hers.

The first survivor crept back when Ra was still high in the sky, drawn by the smoke and the smell of roasting meat. He peered from the ruins, then gave a cry.

'The Golden One! The Golden One has returned!' He ran to Narmer and prostrated himself. 'It's a miracle!' he cried joyfully. 'Ra be praised! Our Golden One back again! And walking!'

Narmer touched the man gently on the shoulder to indicate that he should rise. 'It's Rintup the rope maker, isn't it?'

'Yes, Lord.' Rintup stood up and stared around the camp — at the donkeys munching the grass that grew among the ruins, at the cat sprawled across Nitho's lap —

as though trying to take in these new wonders. He gave a reluctant bow to Hawk, then turned back to Narmer. 'Have you come to save us, Lord? To give us back our town?'

It was as though the past three years had never happened, Narmer realised. 'I will try,' he said honestly. He gestured to Portho to give the man some meat.

All afternoon more survivors came to join them, first peering from the shadows at the fire and the donkeys, then coming out boldly when they saw who was there, or fetching friends to join them, till finally more than a dozen were crouched around the fire. All were men. Those whose families had escaped too had left them in safety, hidden in the hills.

'Our Golden One,' said one of them, gazing at Narmer as though he feared he would vanish like a desert mirage. He'd farmed the fields behind the palace, Narmer remembered.

Each person had a story, a family tragedy — a child pierced by a Yebu spear, a wife torn away screaming, an aged parent led into slavery, their hands bound, their heads bowed. They had stories of escape, of hiding, of scavenging in the remnants of once productive fields, living on lotus roots or bulrush shoots or whatever animals they could trap.

'And always knowing that one day,' said Hierotep, 'the Yebu men may come again, and try to take us too.'

'No,' said Narmer calmly.

The man stared. The others stared too. Nitho looked up from the rock where she was baking fresh flatbread. She'd put on her male clothes again, the scarf over her face. Bast sat close by, a charred gazelle hoof between her paws.

Hawk snorted. He seemed to have regained some of his confidence with others around. 'No? How will you stop them? How can a handful of men defend a ruined town? We don't even have city walls any more.'

'We won't defend,' said Narmer firmly. 'We will attack.'

Hawk chuckled in disbelief. 'A fine boast, and an empty one.' He brushed the crumbs from his dinner into the fire. 'I never took you for a fool, brother.'

'He's no fool!' said Nitho hotly. 'He left here a cripple. Now he's Ur's richest merchant, admired by the whole city!' Which was true, thought Narmer — though it left out the fact that it was because he'd been adopted by the Trader.

'Travellers' boasts,' returned Hawk scornfully. 'How convenient that there is no way to check if they're true. And even if they are … how can a trader defeat a town like Yebu? Swap victory for a bag of spices?'

The men gazed from Hawk to Narmer. Suddenly Hierotep bowed, as low as he would have to Narmer's father. 'Prince Narmer fought the crocodile and won. He has crossed the Endless Desert and lived. He has tamed the wild donkeys and the wildcats. The Golden One can do anything.'

'What is your plan, Lord?' asked Rintup.

'I don't know yet,' admitted Narmer. 'But I promise you this: by the next flood our people will be free.'

It was impossible to sleep. There was too much to think about. His father's bones, washed away by the River, with no grave goods or spells to speed safely him to the Afterlife. His people, serving masters in Yebu. His brother, who had betrayed not only Narmer himself but also all of Thinis, still king in name, if not fact.

Nitho, asleep in her tent nearby.

The people trusted him — much more than they trusted their king. But what had Narmer to give them? Had his promise been an empty boast, as Hawk had said? A way of saying to his brother, 'You lost the kingdom, but I can gain it back?'

He wished Nammu were here. He needed the old trader's wisdom, and his experience. Or an oracle, he thought with a smile. One who could tell him how a handful of men could conquer a town and set their people free. If only there were a real oracle in the wadi — even one like Nitho who would make him realise things he already knew.

How could they break through the walls of Yebu? Only two things destroyed mud walls: an army and the River, and only working together. But he had only a handful of men — and as for the River, it answered to no man's orders ...

Narmer sat up so suddenly that Bast — who had been sleeping on his feet — hissed and stalked off into the darkness, annoyed.

He'd been a fool! He already knew how to make a river move! But could he make it move to Yebu?

He'd never get to sleep now. He stretched silently, then walked into the old First Courtyard.

The moonlight shone onto the water of the pool. It was almost possible to believe that if he shut his eyes, when he opened them his father would be on his chair, and Seknut fussing in the shadows ...

He had to put the hurt aside. Pain made it hard to think. He had to plan, to think of Thinis, not himself ...

'Are you all right?'

It was Nitho. Of course it was Nitho, thought Narmer. She still wore her boy's clothes, but had left off her scarf, and her hair hung to her shoulders. He had a sudden longing to touch it, to feel its softness. 'Whenever I need you, you're there,' he said to her.

He wondered if she was blushing in the darkness. 'There were too many mice in there to sleep. One of them just ran up my leg. Where were you going?'

'Nowhere. Just trying to think.' He hesitated. 'I have an idea.'

He outlined it to her, watched her face grow thoughtful in the moonlight.

'It might work.'

'Only "might"?'

'What do you want me to tell you?'

'The truth. You always do anyway,' said Narmer.

'The truth is that I think you have a chance. I've seen Yebu, remember. We came that way on our last visit.'

'I didn't know,' said Narmer, surprised. He had never been there himself.

Nitho laughed. 'You should know by now that traders don't mention doing business with a town's enemies. We went to Yebu before Thinis. They gave us a good price for our myrrh too. Yebu has higher walls than Thinis had. But I'm sure the River is on higher ground than the town. It's only the drifts of silt deposited by the River that keep the town safe. I can draw you a map tomorrow.'

'And if we can cut a canal through the silt, the River will move the walls.' Narmer smiled at her. Things no longer seemed so impossible. 'All we need now is an army.'

Suddenly Nitho screamed. It was a small scream, more a muffled shriek.

'What is it?'

Nitho reached down into her tunic and brought up a struggling mouse. She shuddered. 'I hate the things! I'd rather face the whole Yebu army than —' She stopped, as the cat slunk into the courtyard. Bast gazed at the mice scurrying across the ground.

And then she pounced. Once, twice, three times, then again and again, leaping, jumping, prancing across the courtyard, grabbing and gulping and snatching and crunching ... Narmer stared, half disgusted, half fascinated, till at last there were no more mice to be seen. The cat sat in the middle of the courtyard and began to wash herself. She wore an expression that Narmer had never seen before: the look of a cat who had eaten a whole bellyful of mice. And who was already dreaming of doing exactly the same thing again.

'Ugh,' said Nitho. She spoke to the cat sternly. 'If you're thinking of coming into my tent now you can forget it.'

Bast took no notice. She lifted another paw and began to wipe her whiskers. Narmer laughed.

'Time to sleep,' said Nitho softly. She vanished through the shadows, back to her tent.

I should sleep now too, thought Narmer. Weariness was finally beginning to seep into him. If I were king, he decided, as he lay in his sleeping cloak in the now mouse-free darkness, I'd have a tame cat for every silo in the land.

If I were king ...

CHAPTER 29

Ra's chariot was sailing above the River mists the next morning when Narmer woke. He went out into the courtyard to see a flock of herons wheel above him, then land in the shallows.

Narmer stretched. The town might be ruins, the fields destroyed, but this land was his heart. Every scent this morning welcomed him home.

And suddenly, as he looked across his land, he made another decision.

Nid had already stirred up the fire. The ragged Thinis survivors were huddled around it. As Narmer approached they looked up at him hopefully.

My people, thought Narmer, as he gave the orders for the day. Some men were to set fish traps, others to collect wood. Others were to start repairing a couple of the houses, so their families could move back in.

'And what will my noble brother do today?' It was Hawk. Once more he eyed Narmer's tunic, the amulet from Punt. 'Has the Golden One decided yet how to destroy Yebu for us?'

Narmer looked at him calmly. 'Yes, I have.'

'What?' Hawk gave a grunt of derision. He looked around at the watching men. 'Listen to the fool, then. Your so-called Golden One. He can make you an army out of ashes.'

'Not a fool. A trader. I am going to Min to bargain for an army.'

This was the biggest trade deal of his life. An army in exchange for ... what? A vision? Knowledge of what life along the River could be, in a new age of trade and farming. The donkeys, the metal ploughs, even the cat, were symbols that Narmer could do what he promised.

Four of them made the journey: Narmer, Nitho, Jod and Nid. Portho stayed behind, supposedly to start teaching the Thinis survivors how to use the metal-tipped spears. In reality he was keeping an eye on Hawk.

'Don't trust him,' Nitho had said as they were preparing to leave.

Narmer shrugged. 'What can he do?'

'Go to the Yebu king. Betray us.'

'How? Say that an army of rags and dust is coming to attack him? He'd laugh. As long as Hawk doesn't know the plan there is nothing he can do. Besides ...' Narmer hesitated.

'What?'

'Hawk is the king. He wanted to be king badly enough once to try to kill for it. Maybe he wants it badly enough again.'

'He doesn't deserve to be king!' said Nitho fiercely.

'But he is. He was consecrated as my father's heir in the Temple of Horus. He is king before the gods.'

'The gods took his town from him too,' said Nitho drily.

Narmer met her gaze. 'While my brother lives, he is king.'

'So after all this is over you'll go back to Ur? Live there as though none of this ever happened?'

'I don't know,' confessed Narmer. He hesitated. 'You could go back if you like, before the fighting starts. And take the others.'

Nitho snorted.

Though smaller, Min was so like Thinis had once been that Narmer felt a shiver across his skin. The same mud walls, the same wide main street, the same bakers' ovens and carpenters' shops. Even the colonnades of the palace were the same, their columns made of tall bundles of reeds encased in mud.

Once he would have taken it for granted that every town looked like this. Now he had seen enough strangeness to be struck by how similar this town was to the one where he'd grown up.

Narmer felt memories well up. He forced himself to concentrate as he strode into the Royal Courtyard, with Nitho, Nid and Jod behind him. Bast stalked beside them, as though Narmer commanded her. In reality, Narmer knew, she was hoping for some grilled quail. But she looked impressive nonetheless.

The King of Min was seated on his royal chair. The Royal Courtyard was smaller than the one at Thinis, but there was a lotus pool, the sycamore and carob trees, the bougainvillea.

Narmer bowed, as he would have to his father: the bow of a prince to a king. 'Your Majesty,' he began, 'ruler of great Min, I greet you.'

The King peered down at him, his faded eyes filled with surprise. 'Narmer of Thinis,' he said, his voice hoarse from the sand cough. Around him his family sat too, watching the stranger who had come to plead with their king. 'I thought you were dead — or somewhere in the Endless Desert.' He shrugged, as though they were the same thing. 'My servants have told me why you have come. You cannot be serious.'

'I am, Your Majesty.'

The King shook his head, puzzled. 'Thinis is our enemy, but you say you come in peace. You come in peace, but you ask for our men, to take part in a war. You want an army, but you no longer even have a town. None of this makes sense.'

'Please, noble King.' Narmer fought to find the words he needed. He had the strangest feeling that what he said today might change the world forever, far beyond the fate of a few small towns. 'I have come from the land between the rivers, a land where there are no wars, because their towns have united. By themselves they are small. But together they are too strong for their enemies.'

'Yebu is *your* enemy, not ours.'

'Is it? What if the next time the People of the Sand come they breach *your* walls? The land is drying up. The desert springs are vanishing, the game, the grass. The People of the Sand will be growing desperate. What if Yebu decides to invade *your* town then too? One town alone is vulnerable. Two together are strong.'

The King lifted an eyebrow. 'But Thinis is no more. Not much of an ally if we're attacked. Why should we do your fighting for you?'

Narmer took a deep breath. 'I have an ally greater than either of us. The River.'

'You speak in riddles, like a temple priest.' The King waved a hand as though to dismiss him.

'Please, o noble King. In Sumer, the land where I have been living, there are men who know how to control the rivers. If we cut a channel through the rise behind Yebu we can destroy the walls and flood the whole town.'

The King's washed-out eyes widened. 'Impossible. And what you say is blasphemy! Using the River! The River is a gift from Khnum! Did your father never teach you about Khnum the ram-headed, who sends us the River from his home in the caverns?'

'Yes. My father taught me that. But my foster father taught me that rivers can be tamed.'

The King shook his head. 'Using the River for war ...' he muttered.

'Not just for war, Your Majesty! If we win — *when* we win — I can promise you much more than that. Back in Ur, where I have been living, men build channels called canals to take the water to their fields. They trap the floods and use them as their own. For every field of grain you grow now along the River I can promise you ten more, watered by these canals. I can show you metal harder than stone to use for tools and weapons. I can show you how to build walls so high your town will be safe from invaders. I can show your people how trade with other nations can make everyone who lives along the River rich.

'The towns of Sumer started with no more than we did — a river and some mud. Now they are larger and richer than us by far. But their real treasure is knowledge — knowledge that we can use too — and peace, with towns trading together instead of wasting their wealth in fighting.

'This is what I offer you, great King. Not just a victory over a single town. I offer you peace and riches far beyond any you have known. It's like throwing seeds into shallow water after the flood. Some will rot — but those that root give us abundance.'

Had Narmer convinced the King? The old man just looked puzzled, as though these new ideas were more than he could comprehend. 'It's too dangerous,' he muttered. 'To ally ourselves with a band of fugitives . . .'

'But what is there to lose?' A young man stood up among the seated watchers. He was a few years older than Narmer, and wore the white pleated kilt and gold necklace of a member of the royal family.

The young man turned to the King. 'If this man can make Yebu's walls fall there will be riches for all of us. Slaves, cattle, all the wealth of Yebu for the taking —'

'But that's not . . .' began Narmer, then stopped. Had this prince or his father heard anything he'd said?

But did it matter if they came for plunder, not to fulfil his dream? At least they'd come.

Or would they?

'Father — give me an army. If Prince Narmer's plan fails, if the walls don't fall as he says,' the prince said eagerly, 'We don't attack. We just come home. There is no risk — but so much to gain.'

The King was silent.

Finally he nodded.

CHAPTER 30

Narmer send Nid back to Thinis, to tell Portho to bring the Thinis men south to meet them. Min's king had at last parted with more than a hundred men, as well as his son to lead them under Narmer's command. The King had been surprised when Narmer asked for the men to be armed with shovels, as well as clubs or spears. But he had finally let Narmer have his way. Min's shovels would only be wooden; there weren't enough metal ones from Sumer for everyone.

Now the two armies camped inland from the River, where no fishing boat might see them and raise the alarm. Late that night Narmer sat alone on the cliff above the camp and watched the half moon sail across the River. It was almost as though he had never left. As though the true heart of him had been waiting, sleeping, till he could be Prince of the River again. As though the River itself gave him strength, sending its power coursing through his body.

Now he had the men. He had his plan. But would it be enough? Or was he leading what remained of his people to defeat and death?

If only they didn't keep calling me the Golden One, he thought. They think the Golden One can do anything, even destroy the walls of Yebu. Have they made me believe it?

What do I know of battles? A few skirmishes against the People of the Sand with my father. Stories of war told after a feast. And yet I took command without a second thought ...

Someone walked up the hill towards him. He didn't turn. He'd know that limping stride anywhere.

'You didn't eat.'

'I'm not hungry.'

Nitho ignored his remark. She handed him a chunk of charred ostrich wrapped in flatbread then sat down beside him. 'So, it's a two-day march to Yebu — you plan to start out in the morning?'

Narmer took a mouthful of food, then nodded. 'There'll be a full moon. We'll need moonlight to be able to dig at night.'

Nitho was silent a moment. Then she said, 'I've been talking to Jod and the others. Wait two days before you march. Two days less moon won't matter.'

He turned to her, puzzled. 'Why wait?' He tried to smile. 'You haven't had a dream, have you? Or met an oracle in the wadi?'

'No.' Nitho hesitated, then said in a rush, 'Let me go ahead, with Jod and Nid. The donkeys too.'

'But —'

'No. let me finish. Jod and Nid and I will go as traders.' He caught her grin in the moonlight. 'That won't be hard. We *are* traders. No danger, no reason to suspect us. But once we're there we can find your people, the slaves taken from Thinis. We'll tell them to arm themselves. Then when you attack from the outside, they can attack from the inside.'

Narmer said nothing.

'I'm right. You know I'm right. The others agree too,' said Nitho.

Narmer nodded slowly. She *was* right. A second attack from within would make all the difference. The Thinis people within the walls would fight for their Golden One too, but if they weren't warned who was attacking they might simply run in the confusion. Or even fight on their masters' side.

But to send Nitho into danger ... This wasn't her battle. Thinis wasn't her town. These were not her people. Nitho was doing this ...

... for me, thought Narmer. Just as she made the journey back here, just as, long ago, she forced me to walk, giving me back my life.

The idea both elated and terrified him.

But this was no time to talk about what might be between them.

'Well?' demanded Nitho impatiently.

Narmer dragged his mind back to duty.

'It's a good plan. But Nid and Jod can go. Not you.'

'Why not?' demanded Nitho.

Narmer was silent. He wanted to say, *Because I can't face losing you.* But there was no way he could say that now. He said instead, 'Because you're a girl.'

Nitho snorted. 'I've been a boy most of my life. Besides, women can fight. Look at the guards in Punt. And I have to be there. Nid and Jod can't speak your language. Not well enough, anyway. And I can sneak around. I can contact the Thinis slaves, if anyone can.'

It was true.

'Besides,' added Nitho lightly, 'I'm not one of your subjects, o Golden One. I'm setting out with the others tomorrow no matter what you say.'

Narmer took her hand. 'Nitho … please! It's too dangerous! Is there any way at all I can convince you not to do this? To head back to Sumer, or at least stay here?'

'No,' said Nitho simply. 'If you'll risk yourself in this, then I will too.'

She was right, he realised. No one who knew Nitho could expect her to stay away when those she loved were threatened. Narmer would risk himself for Thinis. She would risk herself for him.

Both of us are doing our duty, thought Narmer. Duty, or … love? Did Nitho feel for him what he felt for her? Not love for a sister or companion. But the sort of love that could only grow around the life, the joy, the cleverness that was Nitho.

'Will you promise me to avoid the fighting, then? Stay in the Yebu guesthouse till it's over?'

He caught a glimpse of Nitho's white teeth as she smiled in the darkness. 'What will you do if I say no? Shut me in the Women's Quarters? Refuse to attack Yebu till I agree?'

'Nitho, I —'

'So this is where you've got to.'

Narmer dropped Nitho's hand abruptly. It was Hawk. He smiled at Narmer. 'Going for another hippo hunt, dear brother?'

'No,' said Narmer shortly.

'The Prince of Min wants to discuss plans. And it wouldn't do to discuss anything without the Golden One.' Hawk's tone was as light as it had ever been.

Narmer stood to go back to his army.

Ra was just rising, pouring his light onto the world, when Nitho, Nid and Jod left the next morning, with the donkeys and all the trade goods except for the weapons, and Bast, well fed on mice, slinking behind them.

Narmer watched them go with mixed feelings. Part of him felt more alive than he ever had before. Part wished he could shove Nitho into a crevice up in the hills, and keep her safe there till it was all over.

But she was right. Without her they might never conquer Yebu.

He was sure the next two days of waiting to follow them would be the hardest of his life.

But to his surprise the days vanished as though Ra had decided to gallop across the sky. For they were the fullest two days Narmer had ever known: explaining what he planned over and over to his men, so there would be no mistakes in the darkness; showing men who had never fought with anything more than a club how to use spears or javelins.

Even more fugitives joined them now, creeping in from the hills — not just men from Thinis, but also outcasts from other towns, escaped slaves, two People of the Sand banished from their tribe for some crime or quarrel — all hoping that if they joined the winning side they might gain a better future for themselves as well.

The army was nearly two hundred strong now. Not enough to win an ordinary battle against Yebu, thought Narmer, even if all the Thinis slaves were able to fight as well. But enough to win in darkness and confusion, with the River on their side.

Perhaps.

The army left in the predawn light, with no one to see them go except the water birds, already wading through the shallows.

The men from Min carried flint spears, clubs or axes and bread and dried beans and fish from home. The Thinis men were armed with the new bronze weapons, and what little food they had — lily tubers and reed stems and the small number of fish they'd been able to smoke on their tiny, hidden fires. There would be no way to hunt unobserved as they neared Yebu.

And every man carried a spade.

The land flattened out as they neared the marshes of Yebu. The soil began to smell of rotting greenery and bird droppings, lacking Thinis's tang of rock and sand and desert wind. But the men marched with good cheer — the Min men and other outsiders dreaming of plunder, the men of Thinis hoping to regain their town, their farms, or the loved ones taken as Yebu's slaves.

And Narmer rejoiced too. The scents of sand and River, the sound of plovers yelling at the dawn, the startled flutter of an ostrich — all were familiar aspects of home that he'd almost forgotten. And somehow leading an army felt like putting on an old sandal made to fit his foot.

Up until now they had followed the River, but keeping far enough away not to be spotted by passing fishermen. But as soon as they neared Yebu Narmer led the men into the marshland. It was much slower going, but the chance of being seen from the water was just too great. Yet birds still rose in great shrieking clouds as they approached and frogs croaked in an agony of alarm.

Finally Narmer raised an arm to signal everyone to halt. 'We'll wait here till it gets darker, and the birds are asleep. We're too near Yebu now to risk being heard.'

The men spread out, looking for logs to sit on in the dampness, pulling out their pouches of food. Narmer went from one group to another, checking all had enough to eat, a place to sit.

'We're fine, lad — I mean Lord,' one of the older Min men said gruffly. The man cast a look at his own prince, already eating the food his servant had put out for him. 'But we thank you for asking. Now, go and eat yourself. This army'll be nothing if you faint from hunger.'

Narmer gave the man a grin and looked around him. The best spots had all been taken. But there was a log a little way from the others. He headed over to it —

'Don't move.'

It was Hawk's voice.

Narmer froze. Something whirled past his face, almost grazing him. It was a spear. It landed in the soft earth, almost at his feet.

The marsh came alive. Something thrashed next to the log he had been about to sit on. A crocodile, Narmer realised. The spear had just missed it. His skin turned cold, as though the mud and River depths from that long-ago attack could find him even here. A twinge of remembered agony ran through his body. The great beast lashed its tail once more, then slithered back into the marsh.

Narmer began to shiver.

'It nearly got you.' Hawk's voice was a casual as ever, as though he were discussing the music of a harp player after dinner. It was always impossible to tell what he was feeling. 'I was aiming for its eye. That's where they say to spear them, isn't it? But I suppose it decided that there were easier meals than you.'

Narmer found his voice. 'We need to warn the men.'

'I think they've been warned already,' said Hawk drily.

Narmer turned. The men were staring at their leader, and at the spot where the crocodile had vanished. One by one they looked around, to check that no other beast was nearby, then slowly went back to their meals.

Narmer felt his legs begin to shake. He sat down quickly on the log. The crocodile's appearance wasn't the only shock he'd just received. 'Thank you.'

Hawk shrugged. He sat down beside Narmer, and took out his own food. Date bread. Hawk must have convinced one of the Min men that the King of Thinis deserved more than papyrus roots and smoke-greased fish.

They ate in silence for a while. 'I'm not going to apologise, you know,' said Hawk at last.

For a moment Narmer thought he meant for missing the crocodile. But Hawk went on. 'You took what was mine. Our father's love. The people's. My position as the heir. All because of what? A child's smile and skill with a spear. No, you robbed me. I only took back what was mine.'

Narmer slapped at a mosquito. The sound carried in the humid air. I must warn the men not to slap them when we begin to walk again, he thought, with half his brain. The other half was yelling at him to feel fury, scorn, to scream at his brother, who had taken his throne and lost his kingdom.

But he couldn't. From the moment he had begun to assemble his army he had felt more alive — more himself — than ever before.

Hawk might be the king. But Narmer was the leader. And underneath all the doubts was the cold certainty that he would raise Thinis once again.

He looked up to find Hawk still watching him. Hawk, who had longed for kingship but had never understood it. Narmer nearly smiled. 'You almost make it sound as though I should be saying sorry to you.'

'No. I was trying to say ...' Hawk shrugged again. 'I think our father made the right decision when he made you heir. Even if it was for the wrong reasons.' He smiled his old smile, which showed nothing of what he felt. 'Or maybe the gods really do talk to a king. If so, they have never spoken to me. You're more a king than I will ever be. Even with no country for your kingdom.'

Narmer tried to think what to say. He had never truly pitied his brother before. 'You're still King of Thinis, not me,' he said at last. 'I'll stay to help rebuild Thinis, to teach the people the things I learnt in Sumer. But then I'll leave.'

Hawk raised an eyebrow, unconvinced. 'Will you really?'

Narmer nodded. 'Hawk, before I ... left ... our father told me something I'll never forget. That to be a king means thinking more about the kingdom than yourself.'

'Ah, is that what I should do, then?' said Hawk lightly. 'Thank you for your wisdom, dear brother. And what does it matter? By tomorrow we may both be dead.' He looked around at the gathering shadows. 'Time to march again?'

Narmer nodded, and began to gather the men.

Dusk gave way to starlight. Finally the moon appeared, a giant loaf of yellow bread on the horizon. Suddenly the reeds gave way to fields. The town of Yebu was before them.

CHAPTER 31

Narmer gazed at the town he meant to destroy. Its walls were mud, like those of Thinis, but the houses here were made of reeds, twisted and plaited together. He could see orchards in the moonlight too, protected like the town by mud walls.

Narmer gestured silently. The army began to move again, skirting the town, up the slight slope behind the fields, then down again. Once again water gleamed in front of them.

Narmer shut his eyes for a quick prayer to any god who might be listening. The plan had all seemed so simple back in Thinis. The River was higher than Yebu, so a canal must bring water down to the town. But now he was here, seeing the dips and rises of the land, it no longer looked as clear. Was there really enough height for the water in this channel to flood the town?

Nitho had said that there was. He had to trust her.

He ordered the men quickly into a line, stretching from the River across the hill. The army began to dig.

The moon climbed up into the sky. The channel was a spade's depth now all the way along, except for a small dyke they had left next to the River.

Narmer raised his hand in a signal. Some of the men began to dig through the dyke as well, while the others made the channel deeper, then deeper still. Spadeful after spadeful, a hundred wooden spade heads slipping as quietly as possible into the damp earth, shifting, moving, lifting …

An owl hooted, deep in the swamp. Narmer glanced up at the sky again. Not long till dawn now, he estimated. Would they make it in time? If the water didn't start to flow along their channel soon the plan was doomed. Their army was doomed too, because daylight would show Yebu the whole of their plan.

If it didn't happen soon …

Narmer stopped digging. The water had begun to flow!

A trickle at first, then a gurgle and then a rush …

'Stand back!' Narmer was afraid his words might carry to the city, but too many of his men were standing by the edge, staring at the surging water. They scrambled to obey him. Within a few breaths the bank that they had been standing on crumbled to pieces and was borne away.

Narmer looked over at Yebu. Would the water reach the walls now that they had cut through the hill?

But even as he watched, the darkness around the walls changed. The water had reached them.

The power of water …

And now they waited, staring down at the high mud walls of Yebu. They looked so tall and strong from here. But more water was rushing around them all the time, as the River changed its course to follow where man had led.

They waited while the moon floated across the sky like a fishing boat on the River. A memory of Nitho, sitting by

Inanna's temple, flared into Narmer's mind. Inanna, goddess of war. Was she angry that Narmer had cheated her of Nitho's offering? A true son of Sumer would be praying to her now for victory. But Narmer had never felt so much a prince of Thinis.

He glanced at Hawk, sitting a little apart from the others, his chin on his knees. What was he thinking? Of glory to come, when he was king of a rich city again?

Or wondering perhaps if his younger brother would steal the throne, once the battle had been won.

King, as Narmer was always meant to be . . .

The thought made his blood stir, like the River stirred when it first tasted the flood. But Narmer thrust the image from his mind. He was doing this for Thinis, for his father, for his people. And when it was over he would become a man of Sumer once again.

Will you? said a voice deep in his heart. Can you really?

Narmer ignored it.

Suddenly the darkness below them began to move. The mud walls shuddered as though they were alive. Their tops began to fall as their bases crumbled into the water.

Narmer leapt to his feet and gave the signal.

His army began to run.

Across dry land at first, then their feet sank into the wet earth and they struggled to keep upright with the swirling water around their knees.

And finally the last of the walls was swept away. Water poured into the town of Yebu in a vast and muddy wave, then flattened out to spread in a shallow tide throughout the city.

'Thinis! Thinis! Thinis! Min! Min! Min!' Narmer's yell echoed across the sleeping town as he leapt across the slippery remnants of the walls.

Or was it sleeping? From inside the town the same yell came back to him: 'Thinis! Thinis!'

Slaves burst out of the courtyards. They ran down the central street, carrying weapons stolen from their masters, or broken chairs or headrests to use as clubs.

Guards yelled from the town gates. They had probably been dozing, thought Narmer, never suspecting that their walls were about to be swept away behind them.

Women shrieked as they found water seeping through their doorways. Children screamed, with water rising from their ankles to their knees, and climbed up on tables, stools, chests, or into their mother's arms, terrified of the churning current in the darkness.

The splashing grew louder as the runaway slaves and the ragged army of Thinis and Min met together inside the gates of Yebu, to make one fighting force.

And then the men of Yebu grabbed their weapons and spilt out into the muddy streets to find the enemy. They pounded towards Narmer's forces. Suddenly they attacked.

The two armies fought in the marketplace, by the crumpled city walls, with water up to their ankles, among the tables of pots, mats and baskets laid out for a day's trading that would never come. The horizon was grey now, not black, but the moon was still brighter than the dawning day.

How do you fight a battle in the semi-darkness? How do you know friend from foe?

225

You keep together, back to back. Those beside you are your countrymen, those in front your foes.

Narmer thrust out with his javelin, felt the hard metal slice into flesh, heard the man in front of him gasp as he collapsed.

Stab, slash. Another fell, and then another. Stab, slash ... Men were dying around him in the darkness, whether friends or enemies he couldn't tell.

Stab, slash.

His feet were wet with mud, with sweat, with blood.

Hawk, suddenly a true king, fought next to him as he never had before, with no thought of himself or of his safety, stabbing with his javelin, his face firm, intent, for once no hidden plan behind it. Portho's great bulk heaved his war club, the enemy falling beneath it like wheat before a sickle.

Stab, slash. More Yebu men fell before them.

There are too many of them, thought Narmer desperately. Far more than I realised.

And how long would the men of Min remain loyal? They were only here for the plunder. How long would it be before they decided this wasn't the easy battle they had hoped for, and fled?

'Narmer! Watch out!' It was Hawk's voice.

Narmer turned. The war club struck his shoulder, not his head. But it was enough to drive him to his knees. The water splashed about him as he struggled to get up, dazed and groping for his javelin. Dimly he sensed the club descending again.

'Narmer!'

Hawk grappled with someone at Narmer's side. Suddenly the club was gone. The man wielding the club was gone as well. His brother's hand hauled him roughly to his feet.

'Hurt?' Hawk grunted.

Narmer staggered, then caught his balance. 'No.'

He should thank his brother for saving his life. Twice in one night . . .

But there was no time to talk. Stab, slash . . . and when he looked again his brother was gone, hidden by the mass of fighting men.

The enemy seemed endless. The collapse of their walls had shocked Yebu for a while, but now they fought as a disciplined group once again.

Slash, stab . . . draw the javelin back and stab again.

Slash, stab. Duck and shift and stab again. Enemy after enemy, endless . . . impossible . . .

They're going to win! thought Narmer with a flash of panic. I was wrong! The flood, the surprise attack . . . they're not enough! Any moment now half our army is going to run . . .

How could he hold them all together? The Min men and the outcasts barely knew his name. How could he rally them again, into a single force?

'Thinis! Min!' he yelled. But the words were almost lost in the noise of battle. Half his breath had gone with fighting.

Here and there ragged shouts answered him, as his men struggled towards their leader. But not enough. Nowhere near enough.

227

Stab, slash … it was impossible to think and fight as well. But he had to think. There had to be a way …

Suddenly a noise pierced the din of battle. A rumbling, splashing sound. Someone yelled, high above the yells of men.

'Narmer! Narmer! Narmer!'

The voice was unmistakable. It was Nitho! Narmer stared. And all around him men stared as well.

Nine donkeys galloped down the main street of Yebu. The other three donkeys galloped behind, each pulling a cart. The first carts ever seen along the River — but not the farm carts Narmer had seen back in Sumer. These carts were only platforms above two wheels. And balanced on each of them, Nid and Jod and Nitho waved their weapons, slashing at the enemy.

'Narmer! Narmer! Narmer!'

Nitho wore her woman's dress and the gold amulet from the Queen. Her head was bare. Her hair streamed behind her, like darkness about the moon, her scar a deep red across her face as she yelled defiance at the enemy.

'Narmer! Narmer! Narmer!'

She was the war goddess, thought Narmer, dressed in gold and white and riding above them all. Savage, determined, impossibly beautiful in the moonlight.

Around him men screamed. Not shrieks of anger or pain this time, but yells of terror, screams of awe. The united mass of Yebu men broke into a hundred frightened individuals.

The men of Thinis gazed in awe too. But for them this was a miracle — a goddess calling out their leader's name.

'Narmer! Narmer! Narmer!'

Once more Narmer's army surged together, their faces dappled with mud and blood.

'Narmer! Narmer! Narmer!'

Even the Min men cried out his name now, as they rushed after the carts to the attack.

Slash, stab . . .

Narmer was vaguely aware of Nitho, Jod and Nid still hovering above them, their javelins stabbing the enemy.

Was Nitho safe? As safe as anyone in this chaos, he thought. At least she was high above the battle. And there was nothing he could do about it now.

'Narmer! Narmer! Narmer!' The battlefield roared with voices as more men took up the cry.

It was easy to tell friend from foe now. The Yebu men were on the run, while Thinis and Min together yelled Narmer's name.

Suddenly Narmer saw a man in front of him, wearing the blue and white headdress of a king. He too was yelling, frantically trying to rally his men.

Narmer let his javelin fall and threw himself onto the King. His one thought now was not to kill, but to stop the killing, to force this man to surrender.

They plunged together, down into the muddy water. For a moment, as the coldness covered his head, Narmer remembered the long-passed battle with the crocodile. But now, as then, he held on. They grappled for a moment, and then he had the King's throat . . .

He struggled up. He took his hands from the throat of the King, then wrenched the man's arms behind his back. 'Surrender!'

The King grunted in pain.

'You can stop the slaughter! Surrender now!'

'And live in slavery?'

'No.' Narmer gasped for breath. A few men still fought around them. But even as he watched most of his men had begun to head into the streets after their fleeing enemies.

Where was Nitho? Yes, there she was, no longer on her cart. The donkeys must finally have been spooked by the noise and blood. They were galloping back down one of the streets. But their job had been done. Safe, he thought. At least she's safe.

'Min! Thinis!' he yelled, as the King continued to struggle next to him. 'To me! To me!'

The battle-dazed men looked round. Some hesitated, their blood still up. But others took up the cry. 'Narmer! Narmer!' One by one the men began to gather round.

Narmer turned back to the King. 'No slavery,' he panted. 'No more dead. An alliance under Thinis's leadership. Do you accept?'

He felt the King's slump of defeat in his arms.

CHAPTER 32

Battles were easier than their aftermath, thought Narmer wearily.

Daylight drenched the battered town of Yebu. The fighting was over. Prisoners stood with bound wrists, ankle-deep in the muddy water that still flowed through the streets. Soon some of his men would march them out into the fields and up the rise, to fill in the channel and build another dyke to keep the River from Yebu.

So much to organise. A kingdom to hold together.

How did you do it? he asked his father.

But even as he helped his men haul up the wounded before they drowned, and drag the corpses to the marketplace for their families to collect, new plans were rising in him, like the yeast in baker's dough. Two towns were stronger than one; four towns made a nation, just as it was in Sumer.

And suddenly a vision burst through his mind: the entire River, united, trading and working as one country, a land of such peace and prosperity that people would talk of it for more than six thousand years.

Meanwhile, all around him joyous reunions were taking place, as the Thinis slaves greeted their loved ones.

'He has saved us! The Golden One has saved us!

'He moved the River! Even the River obeys the Golden One!'

'Your Majesty?

Narmer turned. It was Jod. 'Majesty'? thought Narmer. Jod had always called him 'Master', or 'Young Master' perhaps. 'Majesty' was what you called a king.

'Your brother . . .' said Jod quietly.

They waded through the remnants of the flood. The silt had stained the water so it was impossible to tell what was blood.

Someone had laid his brother on a table in Yebu's marketplace. Perhaps last night the table had held pottery or fresh bread. Now it held the body of a king.

His brother's face looked strangely peaceful. One hand still held his javelin, so that it rested across his breast.

Had he fallen protecting Narmer from the war club? Narmer would never know how his brother had lost his life. But he knew that Hawk had died, finally, as a king.

So now *I'm* king, thought Narmer. No, not king. Yebu's king can rule his town. Min's king will still rule too. Each town we conquer will have its own ruler. But I will be leader of them all.

Pharaoh. The Golden One.

The thought brought no elation. It just seemed right, as though Narmer had slipped on a pair of sandals made to fit his feet.

He gestured to two of his men. 'Carry his body to the palace. Find Berenib, the woman who was his wife. Tell her to dress him with all honour. He is a king, and will be buried as one.'

The energy of battle was seeping away. Nitho will know what to do now, he thought. Nitho can help me organise ...

Nitho ...

Where was she? Why hadn't she come to join him?

He began to wade through the water, avoiding the floating bodies. 'Nitho? Nitho!'

Men cheered him as he passed. Min men, Thinis men: they were all one army now. A group of Thinis slaves bowed low. 'My Lord, thank you! Thank you!'

'Wherever you lead we will follow, my Lord!' yelled one of the Min men.

'The girl on the cart! Find her!' he shouted.

'Yes, my Lord. Anything!'

Narmer rushed through the muddy colonnades. A woman peered at him from a doorway.

'The trader!' he called. 'Have you seen the trader? The girl who rode behind the donkeys? Have you seen her?'

The woman shook her head, her eyes wide with fear.

He entered a courtyard, then another, where two children hid behind a giant pot. He pretended not to see them. No sign of Nitho here.

He made his way slowly back to the marketplace. Where was she?

Suddenly his skin grew cold.

He began to help the men haul up the bodies from the mud again, frantic, his tiredness gone. But now he was looking for one face alone. A scarred face, with a twisted lip, dearer to him than any other could be.

'Hurry!' he yelled desperately. A tide of emptiness washed through him. There was triumph, glory — but no Nitho.

He yelled out her name, as though sheer noise might make her reply. But no voice answered him. Men gathered round him, helping too. Body after body ...

A man's body, its drowned face white except for the mud and a bruise on its head. A boy's body, the clothes so like the boy's dress Nitho had worn that he felt a stab of terror. But she had been wearing a woman's dress —

'Hissssss! Yooowl!'

Narmer spun round. It was Bast. The animal was bedraggled, the black and orange of her coat the colour of mud. She was sitting on a giant basket that had once held fish or barley, batting her paws at a fool who had tried to come too close.

A mass of once-white robes lay slumped beside her.

Narmer felt his breath freeze within his body, then begin to gallop again, like wild camels after rain. At least Nitho hadn't fallen in the water. At least she hadn't drowned.

He splashed towards her and lifted her up against him.

Blood. Blood everywhere, soaking into her dress, dripping over the gold she wore at her wrists and neck. Dried blood, almost black. Fresh blood oozing down her face from a great ripped cut above her eye.

Fresh blood. She was alive!

It was as if his heart had stopped beating, then crashed to life again like a flood surging down a wadi.

He yelled for help, tore a strip from his tunic and pressed it against the cut, then searched for other injuries. A blue bruise on her forehead; her eye would be black tomorrow. But no other wound that he could find.

She would live, then. She *had* to live!

The cat glared at him, as though it were all his fault. And she's right, thought Narmer.

He sat on a nearby table with Nitho on his lap. She *had* to wake up. For a moment his life stretched before of him, a life without Nitho, as dry as the world without the River.

Then her eyes opened. She blinked, confused, and smiled faintly as she recognised him.

'You're safe,' she whispered.

He stroked her muddy cheek. 'Yes.'

'It's over? We won?'

'Yes. Shh, my darling Nitho. All's well. Shh.'

But her eyes stayed stubbornly open.

'What now?' she whispered.

He almost smiled. How could he find the words, at a time like this, for all that was in his mind?

And then he had them.

'Now you will be my queen. You will, won't you?'

She muttered something, too low for him to hear. He bent closer to her mouth.

'Stupid ...' she murmured. And then, 'Of course ... always loved you ...' she added, the words almost lost in the noise around them.

'I love you too,' he said, even though her eyes had drifted shut again. But he knew she heard him, as her fingers clasped his hand.

'Bring our father here,' she whispered. 'Teach them traders' writing. Teach them traders' routes ... Trade ... proper ships along the River ... will bring the River towns together.'

'Yes,' he said. 'But shh now. We can talk about this later. We have all the time in the world.'

'Later ...' she breathed.

She seemed to sleep. But the hand that held his stayed warm and firm.

I always loved you! he thought. My oracle, friend, sister, companion ... queen. How could I rule without you?

He sat there holding her, feeling her heartbeat next to his, listening to the bustle all around: the joyful calling of the Thinis slaves, his men marching the prisoners off with their spades, Jod hurrying towards them — and old Seknut, her face lit up with the widest smile of pride and happiness she had ever given him, hobbling up with clean water and linen. She too was alive, and safe!

But Narmer's eyes fled back to Nitho's injured face. 'You'll be fine in a day or two,' he told her softly, as Seknut, understanding the situation at a glance, began to press a bandage to Nitho's wound. 'And if your face has another scar — well, it was you who told me once that all princesses are beautiful. They'll call you beautiful too, when we are married. And you are.

'We'll teach them to control the River, to bring water to the desert. And we'll bring our father here. Perhaps he can work out other words to write, not just for trading, so that our knowledge can be remembered — and our names will live for six thousand years.

'I will be the pharaoh, and you my queen. The first in my heart. My dearest friend. And when the gods come to judge us in the Afterlife, we'll walk together.'

The following account is written by me, Hesyre, Scribe to the mighty Narmer, first Pharaoh of all Egypt, wearer of the Dual Crown of North and South, who united our land as one Kingdom, diverted the might River Nile, built cities and invented the papyrus on which I write. Our glorious Pharaoh died aged sixty-three while hunting hippopotamus. His great queen Nithotep ruled after him as regent, with their son, Djer. Long may Narmer and Nithotep rule together in the Underworld. Long may their names be remembered.

AUTHOR'S NOTE

This book takes place about 3000 BCE, long before the pyramids of Egypt were built, or Jerusalem, and before Egypt had mummies, scribes, hieroglyphics or irrigation.

When we think of 'ancient Egypt' we think of the pyramids. But the times of the Pharaoh Narmer were 'ancient history' to the builders of the pyramids too. Most of the information you'll find about ancient Egypt is far too modern to be relevant to this book.

Yet five thousand years ago was one of the world's most fascinating times, especially in the Middle East and Egypt, where this book is set, and around the Mediterranean.

It was the beginning of civilisation as we know it now. Instead of being nomads, travelling from place to place gathering wild food, people were learning new ways to farm and starting to build cities, instead of just small villages. In the early days of farming, tribes would camp for months by the fields of grain, waiting for it to ripen, then pick and thresh it — getting rid of the stalks and the husks around the seeds. Then during the colder months of the year they'd have to lug around all the wheat they'd gathered. So slowly people decided to stay put instead of wandering around — and the world's first settlements grew up around the wild wheat fields.

It was the age of domestication, too, as humans realised that instead of hunting wild animals they could farm them, and train them to work. Such animals included horses, dogs, camels and cats.

The landscape of Egypt and the Middle East was very different from today, with forests, marshland and grasslands instead of today's vast deserts. The deserts in this book would have been smaller than the ones in the same areas today, and probably had more springs and scattered grass where animals could graze. But this also seems to have been a time when these areas were becoming drier, forcing farmers to learn how to irrigate, and more and more nomads to seek moister pastures.

Life was growing harder in other ways too. Now that people were living in one place and their water was becoming polluted with their sewage, they started to catch diseases, especially from the animals they lived so close to — measles from cows, tuberculosis from cows and goats, and influenza from pigs and ducks. In earlier times humans were too spread out for disease to travel from group to group. Now for the first time many illnesses really got a hold on our lives.

Wars grew more serious, as people fought for land near water and there were more people living in one place to fight, though there were still no professional armies. People who owned land — or controlled it — were better off than those who didn't, so for the first time there was a real difference between the wealthy and the poor. Rich people now had slaves captured in battle, or servants: people who owned no land and had to work for someone else for their food.

Above all, this was the time when humans learnt to write down their knowledge, their myths and their history, so that all these new wonders could be passed on to other people they would never meet.

It was possibly the time of greatest change that humanity has known.

NOTES ON THE TEXT

Cats: Wildcats were probably first domesticated in Egypt about six thousand years ago, to help control mice and rats. These wildcats were much larger than today's house cats. They replaced the earlier pest control species — ferrets, one of the earliest domesticated animals.

Cubit: About half a metre.

Donkeys: The donkeys in this book were really wild asses, or onagers. I have used the word 'donkey' because it's more familiar.

Wild asses were possibly first domesticated near Sumer. Early carts and perhaps chariots were used in Ur too, long before horses were tamed in that area. Chariots, carts and riding didn't really catch on until horses were domesticated. This happened around 3500 BCE, but far from the Middle East, probably by herders in what's now the Ukraine, who had already been riding reindeer and using them to pull sleighs, but started to use horses instead. The idea of riding and taming horses spread via horse-riding nomads from the high steppelands of central Asia into central and western Europe and then down into the Middle East between 3000 and 2000 BCE.

Ka'naan: This was later to become the holy land of the Israelites. The ancient Egyptians used the word *ka'naan* or *kan'an* to refer to merchants, or traders.

Medicine: Quite a few ancient Egyptian medical documents survive. The ancient Egyptians and Sumerians had skilled doctors, though many illnesses were treated with spells and prayers too. They used plants like poppy, garlic, chamomile, artemisia, deadly nightshade, camphor, caraway, frankincense, myrrh, saffron, spearmint, turmeric, henna, lavender, gum Arabic and rose oil to stop pain or cure or prevent diseases. Often medicines were mixed with vinegar, flour, egg white or milk and applied to the patient's shaved head. Other treatments were given through the mouth or nose or other bodily openings.

Some ancient Egyptians, like Narmer and Nitho, lived well into their sixties. But ordinary workers were lucky to live more than thirty-five years, and water-borne diseases from the River and parasites from animals were common. Many people also suffered from breathing difficulties such as the sand cough, caused by the clouds of irritating dust and sand from the desert. Eye diseases were common too, but the eye cosmetics used by wealthy people may have helped prevent them.

Narmer: Narmer (also known as Menes, a name used by later historians, or Aha or Catfish), the king who unified Egypt into one great kingdom, his brother Hawk, his father King Scorpion and his wife and queen Nithotep were real people, though little is known about them. Some theories say that Menes, Narmer and Aha were two or even three kings, not one. But most accept that these were three different names for the one king, since ancient Egyptian kings took new titles when they ascended the throne. And all agree that he was — or they were — the first of the pharaohs.

We know nothing about Narmer's early life before he became pharaoh. I invented the crocodile attack, though Narmer did seem to have a reverence for crocodiles. But there is no evidence that he was ever crippled.

Much of what we *do* know about Narmer comes from the Narmer Palette. A palette was a big plate or dish used for mixing cosmetics. This one was placed in Narmer's tomb as a record of his great deeds as king — mostly his military victories. Archaeologists still haven't been able to translate much of it. Perhaps it never will be translated, and we will never know the meaning of some of those ancient symbols, or the names of the cities that Narmer conquered.

Narmer founded the city of Crocodopolis, and dammed the Nile to build the city of Memphis, twenty-eight kilometres south of modern-day Cairo on an island on the Nile River, which he made his capital.

Narmer's kingdom eventually extended from the delta to the first cataract on the Nile, and he sent ambassadors to Ka'naan (the Biblical land of Canaan) and Phoenicia. (See the map on page iv.) The land along the Nile was divided into districts ruled by governors, appointed by Narmer, who also collected taxes and were in charge of draining and irrigating the fields with canals and maintaining the dykes that protected orchards and houses.

Narmer had two wives, Queen Berenib or Bener-ib, and Nithotep, or Neithotepe, who was the mother of

Narmer's only son and heir, Djer. After Narmer died, Nithotep became regent until Djer came of age and could rule Egypt alone. Narmer died when he was sixty-three years old after being attacked either by wild dogs and crocodiles or by a hippopotamus.

Nitho: We don't know where Nithotep came from, or anything else about her. It's sometimes thought that she might have been a princess from the delta whom Narmer married to ally himself with that area. But there's no evidence for that. She must have been a strong woman to rule the new empire by herself after Narmer's death. Her tomb is at Naqada.

Pharaoh: The word 'pharaoh' (which means 'great house') wasn't used until about 1458 BCE. But as it was used for so long as the title of the Egyptian great kings, I've used it in this book.

Pillows: The Egyptians used headrests made of stone, ivory or wood instead of pillows, as some African peoples still do today. The headrests may have had cushions on them too, but we don't know for sure.

Punt: The land of Punt is mentioned often in ancient Egyptian papyrus, but no one really knows where it was, or when trading between the two countries began. It was probably on the Red Sea in eastern Africa, possibly south of Nubia. One likely area is modern-day Ethiopia, which is where I decided to locate it in the map on page iv. Eritrea and Somalia are also possibilities.

There is a famous account of a trading mission to Punt in the time of Queen Hatshepsut (Fifteenth Dynasty, or mid-1400s BCE). I have taken the items offered to the Trader in Punt from the record of trading goods in Queen Hatshepsut's mortuary temple at Deir el-Bahri. No one knows, though, what khesyt wood is, or where green gold comes from. But the colour of gold ore varies in different parts of the world, as natural gold is always alloyed, or mixed, with other minerals, usually silver. But sometimes it appears dark red, orange, or the classic 'gold' we imagine it to always be.

There are legends that the Queen of Sheba — who visited King Solomon in the Bible — may have come from Punt, or that Punt was a nation ruled by women, like the Amazons in Greek mythology.

The River: The people of ancient Egypt simply called the Nile 'the River'. It was the only one in their world, and needed no other name. The ancient Egyptians even referred to themselves as 'Black Landers' after the black silt from the River.

Seasons in ancient Egypt and Ur: The people of both ancient Egypt and Ur based their seasons on what needed to be done on their farms.

Ancient Egypt had three seasons of four months each. Each month contained thirty days, which is the time it takes for the moon to go from 'new moon' to 'full moon' and back again. There was the Season of Flood or Inundation (Akhet), from midsummer to autumn, when the far-off snows melted and their water surged down the Nile. Then there was the Season of Emergence (Proyet), when new shoots emerged from the rich new mud that the River had brought. This was from autumn to winter. Then there was the Season of Harvest, or summer (Shomu), which lasted from our February to our June. There were also five extra days each year for feasting.

Ur's calendar was based on when their rivers flooded too, and what needed to be done on their farms. Their most important celebrations were the autumn and spring equinoxes. Winter was their most important growing season, as in Egypt, and the autumn equinox was the beginning of their farming year. Spring to summer was the time when the Tigris and Euphrates Rivers flooded. (Their floodwaters didn't have as far to come as the Nile did.) The canals filled with water, and the fields were flooded to remove excess salt and to bring new fertile silt. Autumn was the time of ploughing, and winter was the time for sowing and growing crops. Harvest began in spring, before the floods, and grain and straw were cut, threshed and stored throughout summer.

Sumer: Sumer was the area near the Persian Gulf between the Tigris and the Euphrates Rivers. It was part of the 'fertile crescent', where the first grains were grown and where farming began, ten to twelve thousand years ago, after the last Ice Age. (Farming developed independently in Southeast Asia, India and Pakistan, and South America.)

The Sumerians arrived in about 4000 BCE and took the land from the people already there. At the time when this book is set there were at least twelve independent city states, including Ur, Uruk, Kish and Lagash.

The great civilisation of Sumer probably influenced ancient Egypt greatly. But Egypt's writing, dress, ideas of kingship, administration, theories of astronomy, their detailed sky charts and many other achievements were still very much their own. The Sumerians invented wooden wheels, ploughs and oars for their ships. And in this book the Trader brings his 'trader's language' to Egypt, a system of writing known as cuneiform (from the Latin word *cuneus*, meaning 'wedge'), consisting of wedge-shaped counting marks made on clay tablets. In fact the earliest writing ever found is Egyptian, from over five thousand years ago, though it's possible that still earlier writing will eventually be found somewhere else. We may never know where many ideas originated.

Sumerian gods: Inanna was the Sumerian goddess of fertility, love, wisdom and war. She was the daughter of the sky god An and the moon god Nan. Nanna was the creator of the universe, and both male and female at the same time.

Thinis: We know very little about Thinis — not even exactly where it was. We do know that it was somewhere in Upper Egypt, probably on the western bank of the Nile, with a graveyard on the other side, and that it was where Narmer came from and where his father ruled.

We don't know how large it was either. I've assumed it had one or two thousand people, but I may be way off the mark. There is some evidence that there were 120,000 men (women and children weren't counted) living in the land that Narmer eventually controlled.

Tigris and Euphrates: These are the rivers' Greek names, as well as their modern names. But I have used them because they're easier for modern readers.

Trade: Few ancient Egyptians travelled much; most never even left their district. But we know there was trade with Sumer, as well as with Ka'naan, where early Egyptian pottery has been found, and that lapis lazuli may have come from as far away as modern Pakistan. Recent satellite photography has found traces of ancient dirt roads across the fertile plains of modern-day northern Iraq, Syria and Turkey. These ancient highways show us that even five thousand years ago people traded from town to town. Smaller roads were probably used by farmers and herders to take their produce to the towns and their animals to new pasture.

Ur: The town of Ur was in what's now southern Iraq, west of the Euphrates River. It was one of the world's first cities.

People lived in Ur from about 5000 BCE. It would have been a tiny farming village to begin with, then, as the area grew drier and people learnt how to dig canals to bring water to their fields from the rivers, the town would have become larger and larger, supporting potters and merchants and other trades. Back in Narmer's time Ur was much closer to the sea that it is now (the Persian Gulf has shrunk), so it was an excellent trading base before roads crossed the lands. Merchants like the Trader could travel up and down the rivers or across the sea, though there were trading routes overland as well.

No one really knows how many people lived in Ur in Narmer's day, but one estimate is about 24,000. It was a great city at that time, but probably reached its greatest glory from about 2600 BCE, when the kings of Ur became rulers of all Sumer, through to the reign of King Ur-Nammu (2112–2094 BCE), who gave the world the first written code of laws. By then Ur contained around 65,000 people and was probably the largest city in the world. In this era grand temples like the Great Ziggurat were built, and glorious palaces. Ur may also have been the original home of the biblical Abraham.

In about 1950 BC Ur was conquered by the Elamites, and later by the Babylonians. As the land around it dried up and the sea receded, in about 500 BCE, Ur was abandoned. The town was slowly covered by sand, though travellers reported finding ancient bricks and other relics there. Archaeologists from the University of Pennsylvania and the British Museum, led by Sir Leonard Woolley, began to excavate it in the 1920s, uncovering rich tombs and jewels, and the remains of the palaces and the Ziggurat.

There has never been a modern town at Ur. Saddam Hussein established a military base near there, and for a while it was impossible for tourists to go there for security reasons.

Viziers: The word 'vizier' is Turkish, and from a much later date than Narmer's Egypt, but I've used it as it best expresses the function of the king's chief assistant. In Narmer's time the vizier was always a member of the royal family.

Wadi: Gully.

Wheels: The first wheels were developed in Mesopotamia about 3500 BCE. Even the great Incan, Aztec, Mayan, Chinese and Indus civilisations didn't know about the wheel till the knowledge was brought from the Middle

East and Europe. The earliest carts and chariots were probably very clumsy, with the wheels attached to the axles. (Most of today's wheels have ball bearings, so they don't need a rotating shaft, just two little steel rings with steel balls encased between them. Wheels with ball bearings turn faster and much more easily than ancient Sumer's wheels did.) The early Sumerians were probably the first people to use wheels to make pots as well. Wheels may have been used in Egypt from Narmer's time onward, possibly an indication of trade with Mesopotamia.

Wild animals: Many animals were found along the Nile in Narmer's day that have long since almost or completely vanished from the area: hippos, crocodiles, scorpions, cobras, ostriches, wolves, antelopes, gazelles, lions, panthers and huge flocks of quail, as well as an enormous variety of water birds.

LIFE IN NARMER'S EGYPT

Most of what we know about 'ancient Egypt' comes from a much later time. But the Narmer Palette, a mace and jar seals that have Narmer's name on them, and a painted ivory label in Nithotep's tomb all give many clues as to the way people lived so far back in history. (Many of the hieroglyphs from Narmer's time haven't been translated yet. We may never know what they say.)

We do know that history was being written down, possibly for the first time. The scribes, or writers, used a mix of ideograms — small pictures — and phonetic symbols, which stand for certain sounds. All our writing today is phonetic; our letters stand for sounds, not things. But when scribes wanted to write Narmer's name, for example, they drew a small fish called a 'nar' and put it over a chisel, pronounced 'mer'.

Most people in Narmer's time were farmers, but hunting and fishing were also important. Wild animals were hunted both for sport and meat, and also to stop animals like hippos from damaging the crops. There were specialist craft workers too. Potters painted and decorated their pots, or carved them with pictures of animals or abstract designs. Other pots were left unglazed so that moisture would seep slowly out of them, which helped keep the milk, beer or water inside cool. Furniture was beautiful as well as useful. There were jewellers and craftsmen who made fine combs, statues of ivory and beautiful furniture. Long before most of the rest of the world, the ancient Egyptians were trying to create things that were lovely, as well as useful.

There were stone workers, too, who made sharp stone blades, axes and stone tools, as well as metal workers using copper and the newly invented and much harder bronze. Most knives and tools were still made of stone, especially those used by poorer people, right up until Roman times. Needles were made from bone, and later bronze.

Houses were mostly rectangular and made of mud bricks, though probably some poorer homes were made of reeds covered in clay. Mud was hauled up from the Nile and mixed with the chaff or straw left after grain had been threshed. The bricks were then shaped in wooden forms and dried in the sun. It rarely rained along the Nile, and the hard bricks lasted well.

A typical house had two to four rooms, a courtyard or flat roof for cooking, with a dirt floor baked so hard by the sun that it could be swept regularly, and a cellar to store things. Dishes and clothes were usually taken to the river to be cleaned.

Rich people had much bigger houses, but they were still made of mud brick, with rooms arranged around courtyards. The floors in most houses were made of packed earth, though richer houses had tiles.

Even in those days, long before the pyramids, Egyptians were digging great tombs for their dead, with underground rooms furnished with everything the dead person had used when they were alive. People took all their belongings with them into the grave because they expected to be reborn in the Afterlife in exactly the same form as they had during their lifetime. A king would be a king, a priest a priest. Poor labourers might only have a hole in the ground as a tomb, but even they were given a crust of bread to hold in their hand to take into the Afterlife. The classic bandage-wrapped mummies were from a much later time, between about 1085 BCE and 945 BCE. But it's likely that the Egyptians of Narmer's time also embalmed their dead, covering their bodies in resin before they were buried.

Farming

While food and other goods could be bought at markets, for reliable fresh food — and home-grown luxury fruits and vegetables — you needed your own farm. Nearly every house had its own vegetable garden and lily pond. Most houses had an orchard too, with mud walls to keep out floodwaters, and depressions around each tree to hold water, which was usually brought to the tree in a large wooden bucket.

In Narmer's time most wealthy people owned land and had it farmed for them. Rich households produced most of their own food and other goods. Men grew wheat, barley or millet for grain; the women ground it in stone querns, made it into dough and baked it into bread, and brewed barley into weak beer. Flax plants were grown to be turned into fibre, then spun into thread, then woven on looms into cloth that could be sewn into clothes. Wool was spun and used for clothes too, and sometimes woven with flax, but knitting wasn't known. Wealthy estates also produced their own leather for shoes, and kept bees for honey and wax candles.

Clothes

Clothes were simple — a short kilt for men, and a dress with straps for women. (Clothes became more complicated later.) Children often went naked, and workers in muddy fields were probably naked too — it's easier to wash skin than clothes when you don't have a washing machine. We don't know if they wore underwear. A triangular loincloth found in one tomb may possibly have been a sort of basic pair of underpants.

In Narmer's time most Egyptians went barefoot. Sandals were for special occasions, or for when the ground was very rough. The king — and possibly members of his family — had their own 'sandal bearer', who carried their sandals in case they wanted to put them on.

Food

Everyone mostly ate bread, fish and vegetables. Wealthy people might have a few more luxuries, but they only ate them occasionally. Vegetables were grown all year round — leeks, onions, garlic, chickpeas, broad beans, radishes, cabbages, endives, cucumbers, peas and raphanus, a wild radish tasting like turnip. Fruits grown included dates, date-like balanites, jujubes, carobs, figs, grapes and tiny dry sycamore figs. Other fruits like olives, apples, mulberries and pomegranates were brought to Egypt much later, and fruits like pears, peaches, almonds and cherries didn't arrive till Roman times, about three thousand years after this book is set. The Egyptians grew other fruits and vegetables, too, that we can't identify these days— probably they weren't very tasty, and so were abandoned when better-tasting crops arrived. People also harvested wild lotus lilies from the River and ate the stems and roots, as well as the tender bases of papyrus. Spices and herbs like cumin, dill, coriander, cinnamon and rosemary were used to flavour food, and honey and syrups made from grape juice, dates, palm sap, figs and carobs were used for sweetening. Food was cooked over wood fires, and sometimes in small clay ovens.

The Egyptians kept cattle, goats and sheep for milk. Their milk was kept in egg-shaped earthenware jars, topped with grass to keep the insects out. It was drunk soon after milking, or kept as sour milk, a sort of yoghurt. In Narmer's day milk was valuable, and would only have been drunk by the king's family, or as part of a feast. Meat was a luxury too, and mostly came from wild animals.

In Narmer's day most people probably ate from shared platters, or big plates or bowls, with everyone sitting on the floor, using bits of flatbread to scoop up the food. Most dishes for everyday use were made of pottery. You had to be rich to afford metal or alabaster or even carved wooden dishes. Plates and spoons were only used for cooking, not eating, as were jugs, ladles and strainers.

A couple of ancient Egyptian recipes

No recipes survive from Narmer's Egypt. But the two that follow may be something like the foods that the first Pharaoh ate.

Date bread: Flatbreads — wheat or other grains and seeds mixed with water and baked into a thin, flat cake — have been around almost as long as humans have been eating grains, at least fourteen thousand years. The Egyptians probably ate the first risen bread; they were among the first beer drinkers too, so they had yeast, and they grew a sort of wheat that would rise when yeast was added to it. (Most flours don't rise when yeast is added. The flour needs to contain gluten for bread to rise; the yeast produces carbon-dioxide gas and the gluten forms little bubbles around the gas. The more bubbles there are, the lighter your bread is.)

But that early risen bread still wasn't much like the bread we know today. If you look at the skulls of middle-aged ancient Egyptians their teeth are worn right down, so the bread probably included lots of bran and bits of stalk and maybe even splinters of stone from when the wheat was ground.

In Narmer's time flour was made from barley or emmer wheat or durah, a kind of millet. Women spent many hours a day grinding the grain, singing or chanting or gossiping to pass the time. The bread was baked in closed ovens. These were probably small, not big baker's ovens that could cook many loaves of bread, which came later. These ovens were basically big hard mud or clay holes. Wood was shoved in and burnt to heat the oven, then the ashes were raked and the bread put in on top, to bake before the oven cooled. Flatbread could be baked on the hot sand, as it is in this book.

Bread was also flavoured with eggs, oil, sesame seed, herbs and fruit. To make date bread, you will need:

½ cup of fresh or dried dates, chopped

1 cup of water

1 teaspoon of fresh or dried yeast (Egyptian yeast first came from beer, which they brewed from dates, barley or palm sap. Bakers would either keep some of their last lot of bread dough to add to the new lot, or mix in yeasty beer.)

6 cups of wholemeal flour (or for a really authentic taste, $5\frac{1}{2}$ cups of flour and $\frac{1}{2}$ cup of grit — but don't try it, it's *very* bad for your teeth!)

Boil the dates in the water till soft. Add more water if it boils away too quickly. Mash the dates, then when the date mash is warm — not hot — add the yeast. When the mixture is bubbling well, add the flour, and more water if needed. Knead it (pinch and roll it) well.

Flatten the mixture till it's about as thick as your hand. Leave it till it doubles in size — which will take an hour or two in a warm place. (Most bread in Narmer's day was flatbread, which cooks fast, not high loaves.) Place it on a greased tray in a very hot oven — as hot as you can make it — and bake it for about fifteen minutes, until it's brown on top. Eat it hot or cold, or use it like the ancient Egyptians did, to scoop up other foods instead of using spoons or forks.

Baked beans with honey: to make these you will need:

3 cups of dried broad beans (other bean varieties wouldn't be brought from South America for another four thousand years)

4 onions, chopped

10 cloves of garlic, chopped

1 tablespoon of honey

1 tablespoon of ground cumin
water, to cover

Place all the ingredients in a pot. The mixture should be well covered with water. Put the lid on then bake in a very, very slow oven for at least six hours — the slower the better. If the beans are very old they may be very tough, and will need to be cooked for a whole day, or even left overnight and given more cooking the next day. But usually six hours is enough. Check every hour or so to see if you need to add more water, as the beans will absorb a lot. The beans are ready when they are soft enough to scoop up with a bit of bread, and all the liquid has been absorbed.

You can also use fresh (or even frozen) broad beans. They will only need cooking for an hour or two. They're best with the loose skins rubbed off before cooking.

2003 The United States, the United Kingdom, other European nations and Australia invade Iraq to prevent President Sudam Hussein from using his weapons of mass destruction against the world. No weapons of mass destruction are found.

I have used the most up-to-date information I can find in writing this book. But as new archaeological discoveries are made we may find that writing, legal codes, domestication of animals and many other things began even earlier than we currently think they did. A lot of material in recent books and on the Internet is already out of date, and no longer accurate.

Notes on this book could fill another whole volume. If you have any other questions please leave a message on my website:

www.jackiefrench.com

Jackie French is a full-time writer who lives in rural New South Wales. Jackie writes fiction and non-fiction for children and adults, and has columns in the print media. Jackie is regarded as one of Australia's most popular children's authors. Her books for children include: *Rain Stones*, shortlisted for the Children's Book Council Children's Book of the Year Award for Younger Readers, 1991; *Walking the Boundaries*, a Notable Book in the CBC Awards, 1994; and *Somewhere Around the Corner*, an Honour Book in the CBC Awards, 1995. *Hitler's Daughter* won the CBC Younger Readers Award in 2000 and a UK National Literacy Association WOW! Award in 2001. *How to Guzzle Your Garden* was also shortlisted for the 2000 CBC Eve Pownall Award for Information Books and in 2002 Jackie won the ACT Book of the Year Award for *In the Blood*. In 2003, *Diary of a Wombat* was named an Honour Book in the CBC Awards and winner of the 2002 Nielsen BookData/ Australian Booksellers Association Book of the Year — the only children's picture book ever to have won such an award. More recently, in 2005 *To the Moon and Back*, which Jackie co-wrote with her husband, Bryan Sullivan, won the CBC Eve Pownall Award for Information Books and *Tom Appleby, Convict Boy, My Dad the Dragon* and *Pete the Sheep* were also named Notable Books. Jackie writes for all ages — from picture books to adult fiction — and across all genres — from humour and history to science fiction.

Visit Jackie's website

www.jackiefrench.com

or

www.harpercollins.com.au/jackiefrench
to subscribe to her monthly newsletter